BOUNDARY PROBLEMS

BOUNDARY PROBLEMS

STORIES

GREG BECHTEL

Freehand Books gratefully acknowledges the support of the Canada Council for the Arts for its publishing program. ¶ Freehand Books, an imprint of Broadview Press Inc., acknowledges the financial support for its publishing program provided by the Government of Canada through the Canada Book Fund.

 Canada Council   Conseil des Arts   Alberta
for the Arts   du Canada   Government

Freehand Books
515 – 815 1st Street sw   Calgary, Alberta   T2P 1N3
www.freehand-books.com

Book orders: LitDistCo
100 Armstrong Avenue   Georgetown, Ontario   L7G 5S4
Telephone: 1-800-591-6250   Fax: 1-800-591-6251
orders@litdistco.ca
www.litdistco.ca

Library and Archives Canada Cataloguing in Publication

Bechtel, Greg, 1971–, author
Boundary problems / Greg Bechtel.

Short stories.
Issued in print and electronic formats.
ISBN 978-1-55481-186-1 (pbk.).
ISBN 978-1-4604-0440-9 (epub).
ISBN 978-1-77048-476-4 (pdf).

I. Title.

PS8603.E418B69 2014   C813'.6   C2013-907503-8
                                           C2013-907504-6

Edited by Barbara Scott and Kelsey Attard
Book design and illustration by Natalie Olsen, Kisscut Design
Author photo by Amanda K. Allen

Printed on FSC recycled paper and bound in Canada

CONTENTS

BLACKBIRD SHUFFLE
(THE MAJOR ARCANA)

A, α

A small black shape flutters up from the ditch in front of the car. He stomps the brake and swerves, the steering slack and useless as the car slides to a halt on the soft shoulder. Coughing on dry grit, he spits out the window and pries his hands off the wheel as the world coalesces through settling dust. He shakes, coughs again, opens the door, and walks to the front of the car.

On the grill, a few sticky feathers, a smear of red. On the ground, a bird. She's female; somehow, he knows this. A miracle of sorts that she wasn't pulped by the highway-speed impact, caught in a wheel-well, dropped to the ground at any point in the hundred-odd metre deceleration. Must have hit and stuck right up to the end. How many variables had to combine just so to lay her out neatly like this, waiting?

Her beak opens and closes silently. Black eyes open wide, blink rapidly, stop, blink again. One wing extends at an unnatural angle, the other flapping weakly, raising small breaths of dust.

He retrieves a cardboard box from the back seat, dumps out the loose papers, and lines the bottom with a facecloth from his pack. Returning, he gently picks her up, lowers her into the box, and places the crude nest in the passenger seat.

He folds himself back into the driver's seat and accelerates onto the road, the drowsy haze of long-distance travel replaced by a new hyper-awareness of his surroundings, a surreal did-that-just-happen sense of dislocation. Nothing has changed. The White Album clicks and cycles over in the tape deck for the fifth time since Thunder Bay, and the sun beats down on the patched two-lane, not even a logging truck to break the monotony of trees. *Idiot strips*, he's heard them called, the narrow fringe of trees left behind to hide clear cuts from highway-drivers.

THE LOVERS (VI)

"I just need a . . ."

"I said, don't."

". . . tissue."

"Shut up and keep your hands on the wheel where I can see them."

"Christ! It's just a goddamn tissue. I'm gonna —" Sneeze. My ears pop. It's not good to hold it in like that, and now I can't breathe through my nose. Fine, then. See if I care.

"Don't talk. Drive," he says.

I try to breathe through my mouth, but my nose drips anyway, thick mucus creeping towards my upper lip. I should shut up. I know that. I should go along with whatever he says at this point. It would be the rational thing to do, but he's being a prick and I can't stand that. Besides, rationality has never been my strong point. If I see something shiny, I pick it up. Sometimes it's sharp, a piece of glass maybe, and I cut myself. Hasn't killed me yet.

I sniffle. "Are you enjoying this? Does the snot-faced look get you off?"

"Which pocket?"

"Huh?"

"The tissue. Where's the tissue?"

"Oh. Front left. Inside."

He leans across my body to retrieve the cellophane-wrapped tissues from my jacket. Reaching into my pocket, he flinches when his hand brushes against my breast. Holding the package between his teeth, he tugs out a tissue with his free hand and holds it gingerly against my face. This isn't going to work.

"Blow."

I blow, and now my face is a mess. He tries to clean me up, and that's even worse. The too-gentle swipe of a used tissue spreads sticky moisture to my left cheek, leaves my chin lightly coated. It's as if he's afraid to touch me.

Of course, I'm a bit nervous too, what with the gun and all.

THE CHARIOT (VII)

Oh fuck.

Goddammotherfuckingsonofabitch. Fuck fuck fuck.

I feel like I've just woken up on somebody's couch after one hell of a party. Can't remember how I got here, and my head's a little off like I'm coming down from something heavy. I want to brush my teeth, get a glass of water, see if anyone will go for breakfast before the hangover gets a grip on my stomach. My head hurts. I want coffee.

Think it through. I'm in a car, and I'm pointing a gun at this woman's head. Jesus fucking Christ. The grip is warm and slippery with sweat, and I feel as if at any moment it might pop out of my hand like a watermelon seed squeezed between thumb and forefinger.

— *Happiness Is a Warm Gun!*

Oh, shut up. What did she ever do to me?

— *This is her fault. Remember that. She's not getting off this time.*

Care to elaborate? Who is she? Better yet, who am I?

Stop. Start there. Focus. Can't look in the mirror . . .

— *Keep your eyes on her. Nothing else.*

. . . but I can look at her. She's small, snot glistening on her face . . .

— *Serves her right.*

. . . and she looks more annoyed than anything. Straight black hair and thin — runway-model, famine-victim thin. Her eyes are dark and wide. Her movements come in quick short bursts, each mirror check, gear shift, or glance at me a sudden flurry of motion followed by perfect stillness. It's more than a little creepy. She's so calm.

— *Not for long.*

The barrel advances. I feel the slight resistance as it touches her temple.

— *Come on. Sweat. How's that feel? You like that?*

Vindictive little bastard, isn't he?

Her grip tightens, hands like claws clamped to the wheel, eyes locked straight ahead. Her first real reaction. The gun retreats, leaving a small round indentation by the hairline. At least she's not smiling. I know her smile, a smug little smirk that's both a challenge and a dismissal. Or would be. If she was smiling.

The car bumps over a pothole and a wave of nausea rises. Clamp the jaw and swallow. Breathe. Focus on dry, empty fields under a clear blue sky. Solid. That dark flicker in the corner of my eye is a trick of the light. There is nothing there. Stay still, dammit.

"What do you want?"

Good question.

"Why don't you tell me?" I say.

"How the hell should I know? All I did was pick up a hitchhiker."

Hitchhiking? Is that my gear in the back? Her voice is steadier than my hand. But my hand's holding the gun and that's got to count for something.

— That's what you think.

Shut up. Either help out or shut up.

I feel my thumb cock the hammer, hear the click. So does she. My lips curl back and upwards, more a baring of teeth than a smile.

"So humour me. Guess. Humouring me would be a very good idea right now."

"Okay, okay . . . Just gimme a second . . ."

— It's an act. Don't fall for it.

STRENGTH (VIII)

"Okay, so you're out here camping and hitchhiking." What does he want me to do, make it up? Okay, I'll make up a story for him. "Maybe you're on the run. Yeah, someone's after you." He's listening, still shaky, and that wobbly smile isn't convincing either of us. How do you calm a scared man with a gun? Show him you're scared.

"Maybe you escaped from prison, or maybe you . . . It doesn't matter. I don't want to know." Avoid unnecessary details. "You've been camping out for a while, so you figure it's safe to move on. Now what you've got to do is get away without being noticed. What you needed was a car, and now you've got one." No response, but he seems calmer. "And you're wondering what's next. What do you do with the driver?"

I regret the words as soon as they're spoken — the pause and nervous swallow are genuine. Finish the thought before he does. "So why not just drop me right here? It'd take me days to get to the nearest town on foot —" He was hitchhiking. Crazy doesn't always mean stupid. "— or you could tie me up and leave me in the ditch. Someone would find me sooner or later. You could even call the police to pick me up after you moved on."

That's it. Give him some control. I ease off the gas and let the car drift towards the side of the road. He's thinking about it.

THE HERMIT (IX)

"You can do better than that." At least I know I was camping. That gear in the back must be mine.

She doesn't respond, just those quick flashes of activity. Look at me. Blink twice. Freeze. Wait. Then quick — check the mirror, glance out each window — then freeze again, this time focused on the road. What is she thinking? No clue.

"You know what I think? I think you know exactly what's going on here."

Nothing. Her hands twitch, but she keeps them on the wheel.

"This time, I know what you are."

There. Right there. A look.

In the window, vague images swim past against her sharp profile: empty fields, farmhouses, silos, grain elevators. No cars. No people. Space and time to spare. Time to figure this out.

THE WHEEL OF FORTUNE (X)

His hands have stopped shaking. Good. My turn.

"Okay, so what am I?"

He giggles, a shrill little sound for such a big guy. Is he losing it? "Oh, you know and I know and we both know you-know-I-know-you-*fucking*-know. Round and round and round we go. It's just so cute, really." No, not hysterical. Just relieved.

"Whatever you say."

He laughs harder.

JUSTICE (XI)

I wipe the tears from my cheeks. God, I needed that.

"So where the hell are we?" Nothing like the direct approach.

"You really have no idea, do you?" Turning to face me, she seems genuinely surprised.

I wait.

She turns back, watches the road. Out the window, sun, more fields, dry dirt. We could be sitting still, watching a continuous-loop tape on a bluescreen. We'll never reach another town, never get across the prairies. Like wandering circles in the woods, the breadcrumb trail erased by scavenging birds. Except there are no woods here, and the road is perfectly straight. Birds or no birds, it's not going anywhere, and I'm still waiting.

"Canada," she says. "West coast is that way." She indicates the road ahead of us with her chin.

Maybe I run a little roadside auto-shop, servicing cross-country vacationers when the vw van breaks down. Keep a special stock for vws because it takes weeks to ship the parts out here and I can charge double price. They don't want to get stuck out here. They're heading for the coast.

She interrupts my reverie, my failed attempts to place myself in the landscape. "You think you've got this all wrapped up, don't you?" Her bursts of movement come faster now, the spaces between them exploding with words. "You think just because you've got a gun you've got everything going for you. But you're not driving the car." Her eyes flick to the rear-view mirror. Back to me. "You don't know where you are. I could be taking you anywhere." More quick glances: the fields, the road, me. "What if we pass a cop car? I see a cop, maybe I drive straight at him." Steering wheel, gun, me. "What would you do then, Mr. I've-got-a-gun? Shoot me?"

Her foot lowers on the gas pedal. As we accelerate, the car starts to shake.

— *Told you so.*

I said. Shut. Up.

She starts out quiet — "You know what I think?" — and builds — "I think you're fucking nuts is what I think. You could be a straight-up psycho, and you've just run out of medication." — louder — "Maybe you've got a problem with women, like that guy in Montreal." — and louder still — "Maybe you think something's messing with your head. Maybe you think *I'm* messing with your head." A pause. Her voice drops low and soft. "And you know what?"

— *Don't ever say I didn't warn you.*

Her eyes settle on mine, and there it is. That smile.

Her foot stays on the gas, and the car keeps accelerating. The little shitbox shouldn't be able to go this fast. The landscape goes nuts in my peripheral vision, doing a freaking jig, but that's not what concerns me. Her eyes, unblinking, aren't just dark. They're black — all pupil, no whites at all. They weren't like that before.

"Maybe you're right," she says.

— *Whatever you do, keep your sights on her.*

Deal.

THE HANGED MAN (XII)

Done. What we've got here is five cards, face down, his cards. (Never let the dealer supply the cards.) And what we're going to do is read them.

Now don't get me wrong. I love card tricks, the sheer narrative ingenuity, the razzle-dazzle and the walloping yarn, the nothing-up-my-sleeve exaggerated gestures, all carefully calculated to provide that sense of random chance, verisimilitude, and wow. But I love straight games too, cards like memories, shuffle them up and deal them back out, only fifty-two (or seventy-eight), but you'll get a different hand every time. And no one, but no one, has a full deck to play with. Even the dealer's got to give them away or there's no game at all.

So this time I shuffled them clean. Didn't stack the deck or deal from the bottom or anything like that, but maybe I peeked a little. No matter. Any serious card-player knows this: the future isn't in the cards — that's the past. What really matters is how you put them together. A million ways to play a hand, none of them right, none of them wrong. And now we're going to turn them over, nice and slow.

"You paying attention?" I say. He doesn't answer, just watches close.

"All right, then." First card.

THE EMPRESS (III)

"Just toss it in the back seat," she says.

"Thanks."

Sometimes they get picky, insist I put my stuff in the trunk like they think I've got hitchhiker cooties or something. Can't really blame them, I guess. Been sleeping in a tent for a while now, no idea how long it's been since my last shower. I can never keep track of the days out here. It's not so much that I don't remember them as that I forget to count. I know it rained this morning and it didn't yesterday. That's about it.

Once, not too long ago, a coyote watched as I warmed up by my fire in a harvested cornfield. The mist hadn't burned off yet, so he was hardly more than a silhouette. I had the gun out, just in case, but when he came closer he seemed more curious than anything. Maybe they don't recognize handguns, or maybe this was just a particularly stupid coyote, but I had a feeling something was going on. He sat and watched for a bit, almost like he was waiting for something, but then he took off. Guess I wasn't what he was looking for.

I remember that, but I couldn't tell you if it was three days ago or three weeks. Doesn't matter really. I've got a ride now, and that's what counts.

DEATH (XIII)

— *Hey! Snap out of it, Princess. Pay attention!*

The present hurts — God, it hurts — but I remember everything now that I remembered then: camping, the rain, the coyote, the pick-up. Still, there are gaps.

— *Fuck the gaps. Don't you see what she's doing?*

"You're seriously messed up," she says, dropping the nervous act.

I'm dripping with sweat, sucking air in huge gasps. Each breath cuts, feels like every exhalation should be a puff of red mist. Out the window, the view keeps dervish-dancing, spinning in wild meditative ecstasy, whirling towards enlightenment. Moroccan dervishes eat live snakes, glass, hot coals; I feel like I've done all three, but somehow enlightenment eludes me at the moment. I'd settle for a glass of water.

"You think you're pretty cool, don't you?"

I can't speak, but I shake my head. I can't tell if she sees my response.

"Drifting along, at one with the land and all that crap. What do you know about the land? You think you know what I am? Give me a break. You don't even know who you are."

She's got a point.

"What do you want from me?" I ask.

TEMPERANCE (XIV)

"I want you to get that goddamn pop-gun out of my face." Soon.

"I'm sorry . . ." His voice cracks. Got to give him some credit. Shaking like a bad case of the DTs, but he's not budging. He tries again. "I . . . I can't do that. I need to know."

He asked for it. Second card.

THE EMPEROR (IV)

As I open the front door and climb in, she looks me up and down, taking in the dirt-streaked jeans, the duffle-coat with its bulging pockets, the navy and white toque with sweat-plastered hair escaping around the edge. I imagine I'm quite a sight.

"Where you heading?"

"That way, looks like," I say, pointing down the road. "That's west, right?"

"Yeah, that's west," she says, and waits.

"I've got no sense of direction."

"Yeah, easy to get mixed up. Trick is to look up every so often." She still hasn't started the car. Maybe she's nervous. She's pretty tiny, and though I'm no towering hulk myself,

I must outweigh her by a good fifty or sixty pounds.

"Look, I understand if you'd rather not give me a ride." I empty my pockets: a pocket knife, some tent pegs, a chocolate bar, a bandana, a bit of rope, a wad of empty freezer bags, and a few coins. The gun digs into the small of my back as I shift in my seat. "You want me to put this away or something?" I say, holding up the knife. "I could put it in my pack."

No response.

"I don't mind."

"Whatever," she says. She looks a bit like a guy I knew once.

She doesn't seem scared, but she doesn't put the car in gear either. I stretch back and stuff the knife to the bottom of my pack. A transport truck blows by, the car shakes, and I'm beginning to think maybe I should get back out and try again. But it's warm in here. I'm still cold and damp from the rain earlier this morning, and there's another cloudbank heading this way.

"Waiting for something?"

"Your seat belt's not done up."

THE DEVIL (XV)

Surfacing to those eyes is like waking under a microscope. If she would just look away. Blink, even. The road's gone now, not even a blur of scenery. Just me and her and those damn eyes.

— *And me.*

Yeah, and you too, whatever the hell you are.

— *Your only friend.*

"What's the matter?" she says. "Having trouble focusing? What do you think you're hopped up on this time? Acid? Mushrooms? Admit it, your brain is seriously fried. Put the gun down."

I've heard of people losing it on acid, but I don't touch that stuff. Do I?

— *Trust me. This is not an acid trip. She wants you to think you're crazy, but you're not.*

Oh, well that's a relief. I'm not crazy, the voice in my head told me so.

"Look at me," she says.

THE TOWER (XVI)

He's hyperventilating.

"Tell me what you see."

"I see..." Again, his voice catches. He clears his throat, winces, and continues. "I see you . . . but there's something not quite — there are these flashes, dark, behind you, like these huge . . ." He waves one hand vaguely at the space above my head, then brings it back to steady the gun. Even with both hands, he can't stop it from shaking.

"You're putting things in my head," he says softly. "Get out of my head." It's heartbreaking, but I can't do that. I almost wish I could.

"You're the one that's out of your head, not me. You think you can get back in there? Good luck, psycho-boy."

Card number three.

THE HIEROPHANT (V)

Once I've done up my seat belt, she starts the car and pulls onto the pitted two-lane. Outside, it starts to rain. Fat drops burst like water balloons on the windshield as I warm my hands over the vent. She drives in silence.

Some people need to chat all the time, need someone to help them deal with all that space, an audience to convince them they exist. Truckers can be like that. They're pretty chatty, full of anecdotes about this or that haul, how they jackknifed on black ice or whatever. Wind 'em up, and they'll talk for hours. Others, they want you to do all the talking.

"My name's . . . uh . . ." Shit. Drawing a blank. "Neil." Neil? Whatever.

She nods.

Up ahead, blotches of sun illuminate the landscape, a patchwork of light and dark in random, blobby patterns. Here it's still raining. The cut fields look like two-day stubble on a very dirty face. I rub my chin, could use a shave. Fish out a leather pouch from my pack.

"You mind?"

"That tobacco?"

"Yeah."

"Roll me one," she says.

I roll two smokes, light them, hand her one. She takes a drag, blows a cloud of smoke directly into my face, and says, "You don't remember a thing, do you?"

She smiles. It's a cold, hard, bright smile.

— *Okay. Now listen up. I am your friend. She is not. This is all you need to know.*

Reach back, slide the gun from my belt, fit my finger to the trigger and point the barrel straight into that smile.

THE STAR (XVII)

Even now, I want nothing so much as to blow it clear off her head. I could do it, too, if I could just stop shaking. It's so cold in here. And she's just sitting there. Smiling.

"You still don't remember, do you?" she says.

"I remember plenty."

THE MOON (XVIII)

"Like what?" I ask, keeping it light, just a little smug.
"Like where the safety is." He flicks it off with his thumb.
Careful now. "Okay, Mr. Memory. Whose car is this?"
C'mon, turn it over.

THE MAGICIAN (I)

I love these long drives. Hours and hours of solitude, no distractions, no nagging weight of unfinished to-do lists. Put myself on automatic and I'm in a space apart, a no-space out-of-time bubble, a climate-controlled transparent womb. Just drive.

It was sunny and clear until I hit that fog bank. Came up thick and fast out of nowhere, lasted about five minutes, then cleared to this light rain, a steady drizzle over empty fields. My friends all told me about the big-sky effect, how you can see for miles and the sky goes on forever. They said Northern Ontario drags on and on and on, trees and rocks, rocks and trees. More rocks. More trees. Once you hit the prairies, though, the sky just opens up and it's like nothing you've ever seen.

That's what they said. They never once mentioned this endless low cloud ceiling, this damp monotony of grey.

Up ahead, a woman stands by the road with her thumb out. Somebody must have dropped her off here. Didn't notice any crossroads. Maybe she's been walking for warmth and some sense of progress, however false. That's what I used to do. She's drenched. I pull over because, hell, I know it sucks to get stuck standing in the rain like that, with all your gear and everything.

THE SUN (XIX)

"My car," he gasps. Oh, he's a fighter all right. This might just work.

"Very good," I say, like he's a little boy who's finally learned to tie his shoes after a series of failed attempts. "Now pay attention. This one's important. Why am I driving your car?"

Last card.

THE HIGH PRIESTESS (II)

Cora says she's just wandering around. She won't be any more specific than that, says she does this when the weather's good. Winters, she usually stops somewhere warm, but mostly she wanders. She says she likes the variety; it's what she's been doing all her life.

"Don't you ever feel like you want to do something more?"

"You mean, like something so they'll remember me when I'm dead?" She smiles. "Not my thing. People remember me or they don't."

"No, that's not it. Not exactly." I'm not sure what I'm trying to say. "I mean something you want to do for yourself. Something that makes a difference."

"Oh," she says. "A difference." Like suddenly I'm making perfect sense. "A dream, you mean. Go out there and fix things. Get some meaning in life." She frowns and falls silent for a bit. "Hey!" she says, brightening. "You want to see a magic trick?"

"Sure."

"Got a penny?"

I dig a penny out of my pocket and hand it over. She holds it up and, with a little flourish, makes it disappear. The usual routine, then. She reaches up behind my ear and pulls out the missing coin.

"Penny for your thoughts," she says. I chuckle politely. "Oops!" She tosses the penny into the air, and it vanishes. Impressive.

She looks around, squinting under the seat, into the creases of the naugahyde upholstery. Then she mimes a big "O!" and her mouth stretches around something white and round. An egg. She's really good at this. She puts the egg down. "Hey, you've got something there. Under your tongue. Let me take a look." I smile indulgently and open my mouth. I've seen this routine before. Something clicks against my teeth. Doesn't feel like an egg. Maybe the penny?

It's a gun, angular and black and pointing at me. She's stopped smiling.

"Stop the car."

I pull over and turn off the engine.

"Get out." If this were a movie, this is where I would do something unexpected, get the jump on her. But it's not, and I don't. We get out of the car. Following instructions, I take the camping gear from the back seat and set it on the gravel. She turns me around and has me kneel by the gear. I feel the muzzle of the gun press into my scalp.

"You wanna live?" she asks. I nod. "Good. Me too. You just stay right there a minute." I hear footsteps crunch across gravel, the slam of the car door. I don't turn around. "You get out there and live a little. Don't lose any of that stuff." The engine starts. "And don't do anything I wouldn't do!" she calls. A spray of spun dirt showers my back as the engine revs, then recedes.

I look down at the gear beside me. A tent, a tarp, and a small camp stove sit in a neat pile. Next to these, a sleeping bag and a backpack. The gun Cora pulled from my mouth lies at the centre of the neatly folded tarp.

I turn and watch as my car shrinks and disappears against the horizon. One hell of a trick, that.

JUDGEMENT (XX)

My car. Her gun. Okay. I just wish I knew why she did this.

— *Trust me. You don't want to know.*

"Look in the mirror," she says.

— *I've got a better idea. Pull the trigger. She's playing you like a kazoo.*

I look in the vanity mirror. Like a window or a TV screen, it shows a featureless grey space dominated by a single figure. A gnarled little man with greasy hair stares back at me. He's filthy, clothes shredded and stained, eyes puffy, bloodshot, and wild. His mouth stretches around the barrel of a blocky black gun, his hands on the grip, one thumb on the trigger. Curled into a tight little ball, he rocks rhythmically back and forth.

I look back to Cora.

"I told you to get out of my head."

"And I told you I'm not in there. I'm right here in front of you. Look closer."

— *Well I'm telling you she's full of shit. You hear that lady? FULL OF SHIT!*

"Sounds scared, doesn't he? Now why do you think that would be?"

Back to the mirror. It shows the same featureless grey, the same little man, but this time the frame expands, pulling back to reveal he's no longer alone. I see nothing but this image, though I can still feel the weight of the gun in my hand, the contours of the passenger seat under my legs, against my side.

At the man's feet, a few paces in front, lies a blackbird. One wing hangs at an awkward angle. Where there should be eyes, only small, ragged holes. It should be dead. These injuries are not new: the blood is congealed, and hard black scabs cover the wounds. A fly lands on the crusted stump of the bird's right wing.

But it moves.

Slowly, the mouth opens and closes. The stump shifts, not enough to disturb the fly, but visible. In slow convulsions, the bird struggles towards the man, so close that, were he to lean forward just a little, he could touch it.

He's got that same wild, terrified expression, the same hunched rocking. In one white-knuckled fist, he holds the gun that was in his mouth, arm thrown out towards the squirming feathered shape as if to ward off an assault. Each time the bird moves, his muscles tense, curling him tighter into that little ball, relaxing only when the movement subsides. His left arm twitches in time with the bird's broken wing.

Two voices I can no longer distinguish speak in unison:

Do it now.

I pull the trigger.

Ψ, ψ. THE FOOL (∅)

He is a mathematical point, a singularity in a smooth, machined darkness. He waits. In the distance, a pinprick of light.

A flash of light and heat behind him, a push harder than anything he could have imagined; cool metal walls heat with the speed of his passage. The distant pinprick of light approaches, opens out, surrounds him. A momentary vision of a car interior flashes past: a man and a woman caught in amber. A soft crack, and the car disappears, replaced by a featureless field of grey. A figure approaches, alone in the grey, a gnarled little man, hunched and rocking, small at first but growing larger.

The face turns towards him, bloodshot eyes shock-widening, pupils large as he is, larger as he passes between them. Bone and tissue part easily. These cavities, this sudden, bright red blood extend a warm, soft welcome, an invitation. Expected, he is the guest of honour. He wants to stay.

Slowing but powerless to stop, he passes through the back of the skull, expanding. Shedding bone fragments, tissue and blood, he continues.

THE WORLD (XXI)

My face is warm, tickled by a slight breeze. A high-pitched whistling draws me up to consciousness.

I open my eyes, blinking and squinting against the red-orange light of the lowering sun. Blocking the light with one hand, I stretch a kink out of my neck. Slowly, the indistinct, streaming points of light in my lap resolve into bits of shattered glass, some dull grey, others silvered and flashing. I straighten gingerly from my slouch, shifting my face into the shade of the sun-visor. On the visor, a neat round hole marks the centre of a ragged, mirror-edged rectangle. Shielding my eyes again, I lift the visor to reveal the source of the whistling: fine cracks spider outward from a hole in the windshield.

Should probably get that fixed before it spreads.

We're driving through a town, but we're going too fast. Small-town cops are just itching to nail the guy treating the main street like a highway. Especially the guy with out-of-province plates.

"It's a ghost town."

"So you don't think we'll get a . . ." Oh. Right. Cora.

I look down, and there it is, indistinct in the shadows beneath the dash, dull, black and weighty. It's just like the one I saw in the mirror; I held it with such conviction. Leaving the gun where it lies, I shift my feet away from that spot. I don't want to touch it. Look out the window instead.

Houses appear less frequently as we leave the town behind. My clothes are cold and clammy with old sweat, but my head and vision are clear. I turn to Cora and see that she's smiling.

It's a calm, self-assured smile. Friendly. I search for any hint of menace, but it's gone. Was it ever there?

"Do you remember?"

"I think so." I shake my head slowly. "I don't know if I get it, but at least I got rid of that little prick."

"He's not gone, you know."

"Well, he's not saying anything, and he never shut up before."

"True, but it's not that easy."

"You call that easy?" I laugh. It feels good to laugh.

"Even so."

We drive and watch the sunset. I feel no need to talk, so I don't. Maybe ten minutes pass this way. Maybe an hour. The sunset seems to go on forever. I look down at the gun. I don't want to, but I lean forward and pick it up, trying to touch it as little as possible, pinching the grip between my thumb and forefinger. It dangles there, nothing more than metal and moulded plastic. But still. I hold it out to Cora.

"I think this is yours."

She keeps driving. As I start to wonder if she heard me, she speaks.

"You remember that talk we had about dreams?"

"Wasn't much of a talk, but yeah."

"Well, here's the thing. Say you got a dream — big, shiny dream. The dream, though, it casts a shadow — big, dark shadow. You feed the dream, starve the shadow. What if you fed them both? Hard to say." She pulls a penny from her pocket and flips it as she speaks. Flip — catch. "So, anyway, say you ignore the shadow." Flip — catch. "What happens? It gets hungry." Flip — catch. "It's got to eat something." Flip — and the penny lands in my lap. "So what's he going to eat, this hungry shadow?"

"Ummm . . ." I pick up the penny.

"Think about it." She folds my hand over the penny and points to the gun. "That's yours. I didn't put it in your mouth.

I took it out." I put the penny in my pocket, the gun in the glove compartment, safety on. "And next time, be careful where you point that thing."

"Deal," I say and lean back with a sigh. "So now what?"

"Oh, I don't know. I think I might get out somewhere along here. Nice country."

She keeps driving, though, and I fall asleep.

Ω, ω

Still no town. The sun has almost set.

Half an hour ago, wheat fields replaced forest and the land abruptly flattened. The speed of the transition has left him disoriented, adrift. The sky opened up just like they said it would, and it's like nothing he's ever seen.

He glances over at the box. The body is still, mouth and eyes open. Is she breathing, or is that just the jostling of the car? He keeps driving as the sun shrinks to a narrow crescent and finally slips below the horizon. Then he drives some more.

Eventually, he pulls over to the gravel shoulder, turns off the engine, extinguishes the headlights, and gets out of the car. A band of deep blue marks the horizon, lingering trace of an invisible sun. Overhead, a dusting of stars spills across the sky from the east. Taking the box from the passenger seat, he climbs into the ditch and sets it down in the tall grass. Then he climbs back to the car, takes out a pouch of tobacco and rolls a cigarette. Putting the pouch away, he hesitates, then tosses a pinch of tobacco into the ditch. Something he read once. He leans back, half-seated on the hood of the car, and smokes his cigarette. As he smokes, he listens to the tick of the cooling motor, the nightsong of insects, the soft crackle of smouldering tobacco when he takes a drag.

It's that quiet.

Climbing into the car, he pauses. He thought he heard something. Birdsong. Perhaps he imagined it.

He turns the key, and the headlights flood asphalt and gravel with electric light. Darkness like wet ink leaps up in response to the lights; silence confronts the engine's whirr. He looks both ways and accelerates onto the highway.

As the taillights diminish, natural light returns. The engine fades in the distance, and the night sounds rise up and up and up, the air filling with rustles, chirps, whistles, and clicks. And other sounds for which there are no words.

THE CONCEPT OF A PHOTON

. . . it is better to regard a particle not as a permanent entity but as an instantaneous event. Sometimes these events form chains that give the illusion of permanent beings — but only in particular circumstances and only for an extremely short period of time in every single case.

— Erwin Schrödinger

The Rabbit shudders and the grinding of steel on steel competes with the rising engine roar as I hit the brakes — too late or unnecessarily, I'll never know. In accordance with some obscure law of inverse proportionality, I have discovered that the engine volume rises as the RPM drops. Check the speedometer: 130 kph. Early March 1995, this is the era of Ontario's abortive photo-radar program. A second or two ago, I thought I saw a camera flash. It's eleven o'clock, the sun long set, and I've been driving since six with that damn muffler getting worse the whole time. Which is to say, that flash could just as easily have been a figment of an increasingly vibration-addled brain.

Bruce warned me about the brakes but said as long as I took it easy they should be fine. The muffler is a surprise, though. When I left Waterloo three days ago, I thought the road noise seemed a bit much. Then again, who expects a borrowed rattle-trap of a Rabbit to float down the 401 in coddled plush silence? No, it's going to rattle and bump and bounce and be a bit loud, and that's par for the course. On the drive to Ottawa, it seemed to be getting worse, but I had no stereo (no benchmark) and therefore no certainty. Now, five hours into the return journey, the hole in the muffler has developed well past the point of a plausible maybe. Two hours ago, a guy passed me on a Harley — some kind of maniac to be on the 401 at this time of year, this time of night — and I couldn't even *hear* him.

For the last while, I've been using the engine-noise/RPM proportionality to my advantage — raising the RPM to lower the noise. Unfortunately, the Rabbit's not a standard, so this strategy has meant driving a little fast. Apparently 130 kph fast, and that's *after* hitting the brakes. Damn. Then again, maybe that wasn't my photo-flash; could've been the guy in front of me, or behind. No way to know until the ticket arrives (or doesn't) at the home of the registered owner. Which, come to think of it, is not yet me.

And though I know I should, I won't mention the photo-flash to Bruce. Rather, I'll drive the rest of the way to Waterloo at an eardrum-battering 110, stumble dizzily into my apartment at two in the morning, and return the Rabbit as soon as I wake up. When Bruce asks how it went, I'll tell him (apologetically) about the brakes and the muffler. It's not like I can complain. At three hundred bucks, the car's still a steal. In the meantime, Bruce will reassure me that mufflers and brake shoes are cheap if you install them yourself, which he'll be happy to do. I will thank him profusely, and I will remain grateful for Bruce's ignorance, which has led to this exchange of a cheap car for a virtually worthless stack of Quantum II assignments.

THIRD YEAR QUANTUM

Our Quantum II exam will ask the following question: "Assuming a single photon of wavelength λ has been sent through the system diagrammed below, what is the probability of detecting that photon on the indicated range?" The mathematical solution to this problem requires two or three pages of calculations (depending on your handwriting), including the derivation and normalizing of an appropriate wave function, the translation of that wave-function into an expression for probability density, and the final calculation of probability on the given range. Ninety percent of the students in the class will take this approach, and about fifty percent of those will get the math right. This answer, though procedurally flawless, will be incorrect.

The correct answer, as Dr. Pintar has proclaimed vigorously and repeatedly throughout the term, is that "There is no such thing as probability for a single measurement!"

I'm working on a particularly difficult Fourier transform when the guy crosses the physics workroom, weaving his way between heavy wooden tables and clunky matching chairs. Each table provides ten or twelve square feet of pitted, varnished white pine upon which to work. In the corner, I hunch amid drifts of shredded eraser, texts piled high and loose papers scattered across half a table. I see the guy but pretend not to. We're the only ones in the room.

"Hey," he says. "Is that the quantum assignment?"

Cornered, I admit his presence and look up. "Yeah," I say.

"Hi, I'm Bruce." Hand extended in greeting, he has a bluff good-natured look about him. Average. Nice leather jacket, short dark hair, a little swarthy. A spray of acne down his neck. Now I recognize him from Quantum II. He always sits in the back, shows up late about half the time and not at all the rest: a fifty percent probability. "Any luck with question #4?"

"It was a bitch. But yeah, I think I got it."

"Mind if I take a look? I'm stuck."

"Sure, no problem." I hand over the sheets in question. "There's a photocopier in the lounge." Bruce thanks me, leaves, and returns five minutes later.

"Hey, thanks man," he says, handing back my originals. "I owe you."

"No problem," I repeat.

FIRST YEAR

At twenty-one years old, I know that physics can (and will) explain everything. I gleefully yet reverently tug at the doors of perception, stepping through into a clockwork universe. Everything here is linear, one dimensional, or at most two. In calculus, we learn the math for three but aren't yet asked to use it in physical applications. Dimensions have new definitions, mathematical as well as spatial. The solution to a physically one-dimensional problem might involve two or three mathematical dimensions, but that isn't so hard to wrap your head around, really. It's just math. There are clear differences between accelerated and non-accelerated frames of reference, the latter yielding accurate results, the former, faulty. Gravity is more or less constant. Waves are physical, ripples across water or down ropes, compressions and rarefactions in air.

In first year, Newton still rules: cause and effect, action and reaction. Predictions are both deterministic and determinate. Given a set of initial conditions, I can tell the future with perfect accuracy. With my newfound kinematics knowledge, I could calculate every possible trajectory for a collection of imaginary point-mass pool balls on a frictionless table with perfect lossless banks. A tedious and time-consuming exercise, but possible. And yet, when I try to play pool based on this knowledge, I lose. Badly.

Bruce continues to "borrow" my assignments for the duration of the term. Every week, regular as clockwork, he finds me in the empty workroom. These are the only times I see him, and we rarely exchange more than three sentences, but I can extrapolate. For example: Bruce seems entirely unaware of standard protocols for cloning. *Cloning* is a widespread and (covertly) accepted practice whereby a group of students divides an assignment into single-question chunks, one per person. Each student takes a question and completes it, then solutions are exchanged. This exchange often occurs in the physics workroom: a crowd of classmates working in tandem, openly passing papers back and forth, copying out answers, consulting. These weekly assignments are worth practically nothing, and the marks are not the point. The point is to learn enough to pass the final, which usually counts for 100%, assuming one has failed the midterm, which most do. Although cloning isn't a practice you would mention to your professor in casual conversation, neither would he be ignorant of its existence. Myself, I don't clone, but that's another story entirely.

From the given set of initial conditions, I construct a probabilistic picture of Bruce:

(1) Bruce is an outsider. An insider would feel no need to thank me (sheepishly) each time he borrowed an assignment. I have the impression Bruce thinks he's cheating. I don't disillusion him.

(2) Bruce is a slacker. Every week, he borrows my assignments at the last minute, and I doubt he understands the answers. I don't mind, as I fully expect him to fail the final. This allows me to feel simultaneously generous and superior, both particle and wave.

(3) Bruce, an outsider who is nonetheless enrolled in an upper-year quantum course, must have transferred in from another department, something science- or math-based. Otherwise, the powers that be would never have let him take it.

(4) Bruce isn't too bright. If he was, he'd realize the assignments weren't worth shit.

Over the following weeks, our exchanges confirm my extrapolations.

Bruce transferred from engineering, sees physics as a sort of home for wayward engineers (like himself), and Bruce-as-engineer neatly explains his clear disinterest in physics. For engineers, physics isn't an end, it's a tool. For physicists, it's more of an exercise in philosophy, an intricate, convoluted, self-referential logic expressible only through arcane mathematical symbologies. Engineers seek the philosopher's stone so they can transform lead into gold. Physicists seek the stone to prove the principle of lead-to-gold transubstantiation. For the physicist, science is both a net cast to catch fragments of reality and a veil to be rent aside, exposing the whole damn unified field at once. We call those interested in the former *experimentalists*, the latter *theoreticians*. Bruce is an engineer.

I am a physicist. Twenty-somethings both, we have already internalized our respective indoctrinations.

SECOND YEAR

At twenty-two, I recognize the hapless naïveté of my first-year understanding. Clockwork, shmockwork. Classical physics doesn't give a damn about electromagnetism, and therefore I don't give a damn about classical physics. I know now that objects can (and usually do) affect each other without ever touching, and that these effects are rarely constant. Now there are fields. Electric and magnetic fields hardly ever sit still, and even gravity's getting fickle. Even so, these fields still behave like stuff I can recognize. Electricity is like water, a liquid with currents (flux) and pressure (voltage). Imagine a garden hose, or what happens when you're in the shower and someone flushes a toilet, and the parallels are immediately obvious. Magnetic and electric fields push (like wind) and pull (like gravity). Like sound from a guitar string, they wave and vibrate. Even inverse-square laws make clear sense in macroscopic, intuitive, everyday terms. If you're close to a fire, you feel the heat; if you're farther away, you don't. Effects diminish over distance. Well, duh.

I begin to imagine the possibility of a larger meta-field that I can *sense* is just around the corner, although I haven't quite apprehended it yet. All of the fields could be stitched together, a series of interpenetrating influences working in subtle counterpoint, the fabled music of the spheres. Just a little more math, and everything will come together like one of those

3000-piece jigsaw puzzles we all did when we were
little. (Didn't we?) All it took was diligence, patience, and
a fine sensitivity to minutely varying shades of blue.
However, in one class, frames of reference are slipping.
Time and space are starting to dilate, and this can
be unsettling.

The pretty girl whose name escapes me at the moment says,
"Bruce says you're really smart." She smiles — flirtatiously,
it seems to me. I'm a little drunk, a little high, and trying to
pretend that all of this is an everyday occurrence. Jen — yes,
that's her name, Jen — wears tight jeans and an AC/DC three-
quarter tee. She's Bruce's girlfriend and the only woman at the
party. Leaning back on the couch, she takes a swig of Coors,
taps ash from her cigarette directly onto the deep pile carpet,
and waits. I fiddle with my ponytail, the one feature I imagine
proclaims my deep inner affinity with Jen and these five guys,
all uniformly clad in jeans and band T-shirts. I wear jeans
and a black turtleneck. We all drink beer from cans. Everyone else brought their own, but Bruce told me the drinks
were on him tonight. Jen's still smiling and waiting for my
response. Stalling, I take another toke as the joint passes for the
third time.

"Aw, he's just saying that," I gamble. Mike, Jeff, Steve, Aloy-
sius, and Bruce watch this exchange in silence, also smiling.
"I'm not so smart," I mumble. "Just obsessive. I think too much."
I don't believe it, of course. At twenty-three, I think I'm a genius.
It will take several more years to disabuse me of this notion.

Bruce laughs. "Don't listen to him. I heard he won some
award."

"Maybe, but what's that good for? Not the money, that's for
damn sure. Piddly couple hundred bucks." I shake my head.

"Not like you and your vans. Now that sounds like some serious cash." Bruce has told me a bit about his current business venture, something to do with buying and selling old vans. I didn't catch the details, though I did see a van up on blocks in the front yard. At the time, I wondered if I was in the right place, the yard so stereotypically white trash, the house run down, paint peeling from wooden slats in white swathes to flake and dust the porch like dandruff. Aloysius greeted me at the door with a handshake, his name, and a half-grunted introduction, then led me upstairs to Bruce and the other guys in what I'm now thinking of as the party room. Here Bruce (to my great relief) conducted a series of more comprehensible introductions, each of which was answered by a corresponding grunt or mumble from the person in question. He also explained a bit about the vans. As it turns out, Bruce is a fairly capable mechanic.

"I mean there's school-smart and there's money-smart," I continue. "And school-smart *costs* you money. You've got to *pay* for it. Not so smart." I feel inordinately clever as this comes out of my mouth. Though I may be a wee bit high, a teensy bit drunk.

"Yeah, it's a knack," says Bruce. "Take this van project, for example. It's gonna clear twenty thousand easy in the first month." He leans back in the formerly-white armchair, spreading his arms expansively. This whole place is formerly-something, a random mix of decades and styles. The deep pile carpet would have been hip in the '70s, probably once had a colour other than ground-ash grey. Beige, maybe. The battered, hand-carved trim around the doors and the chewed-up oak banister speak of decaying elegance, a gradual decline in circumstances. But the overflowing ashtrays on every available surface and the underlying reek of stale smoke say *working class*. Like Bruce and his buddies. By comparison, I feel sheltered, bourgeois, and somehow less real.

I picture Bruce working on one of the vans in the yard. It's a sunny afternoon, a bit brisk, and Bruce has grease and motor oil up to his elbows, a dark smear across his forehead where he wiped away the sweat. Good honest work, and when he takes a break Jen brings him a well-deserved Coors. I am slightly jealous of this picture, though I don't like Coors. Then again, it seems to be going down well enough.

"Hard work, this van thing," says the real Bruce, interrupting my reverie. "Not like the last one. That one was sweet. I tell you about that?"

I shake my head. The other guys' attention starts to drift. Aloysius fiddles with the stereo, hitting play on a new hard-rock tape, indistinguishable from the last. Steve plucks random notes on an unplugged electric guitar. He's pretty high.

"Pop cans," says Bruce.

I blink. Realizing Steve's not the only one who's pretty high right now.

"Pop cans," Bruce repeats, as if this clarifies his meaning. "And a flatbed truck." Jen leaves to get a fresh beer. "Buddy of mine's driving this truck during the week, right? Not his truck, but he's got it in his driveway on the weekend 'cause his boss is too cheap to pay for parking. So I tell him I'll pay three hundred bucks for a day of driving. Of course, he jumps at it." A well-practiced pause. "So we load up the flatbed with cans and take them across the border to Quebec. You know those can-return machines?" I shake my head. Aloysius turns up the stereo and Bruce leans forward, raising his voice to compete with a wailing guitar solo. "Ten cents a pop, and nobody's checking to see what province they're from. A loaded flatbed holds, what, forty thousand cans? That's four thousand bucks for a day's work."

A new vision appears. This time, Bruce wears his leather jacket and a baseball cap, shows up with a full case of beer just as his friend pulls into the driveway with that flatbed. The friend is a typical working-class guy, struggling to make ends meet. He's big, a bit slow-witted but nice enough, and he's always glad to see Bruce. Over a few cans, Bruce lays out his plan to make a few bucks and Screw the Man, and the friend gratefully accepts the role of Little John to Bruce's Robin Hood. I'm envious of this direct-action, no-nonsense model. Me, I'd just think about it. Bruce acts.

"Only two problems." Again, the real Bruce interrupts my imaginary film screening. "I mean, you'd think the problem would be unloading all those cans, but that was nothing. Go to one town, stuff the machine 'til it's full, then move on to the next. Takes a while, what with the extra driving and the time to feed the machines — but still, a good take for a day."

I try to do the math: forty thousand cans, assume two cans per second into the machine, gives twenty thousand seconds, and if you ignore the driving time that works out to . . . Hell, I don't know. Abandoning the math, I nod appreciatively. Any way you count it, that's more money than I've ever made in a day.

"But buddy with the truck, he gets all in a snit, says he wants more cash. And me, I'm like, buddy. It's *my* idea and *I'm* paying the gas. Some people . . ." Bruce leaves the sentence to complete itself: *Some people just don't get it.* I'm thrilled to be part of the silent, implicit *we* of this exchange. Bruce pauses to observe my reaction before continuing. "Buddy ignores me, of course, goes off about how his boss is going to notice the mileage or something, and that's it. Only got three loads in, but sometimes you've just got to walk away."

This is by far the longest conversation I've ever had with Bruce, and the depths revealed are startling. Where before I saw a slacker, I now see a visionary. And not just some pie-in-the-sky dreamer either. Unlike me, Bruce is plainly a down-to-earth, practical visionary. He is Alexander the Great, cutting through all the bullshit with a big old sword, and I'm some poor schmuck getting suckered by the Gordian knot.

If I worked and worked and worked away at that knot, I'd be lucky to get it halfway unravelled by the time Bruce showed up to *chop* that sucker. Maybe I should drop out of school and drive cans.

"Hey, you're out," says Bruce, indicating my empty Coors can. "Jenny, get the man a beer. And bring one for me too? There's a doll."

I nod as the joint comes back around, take a hit, pass it on.

THIRD YEAR

At twenty-two, I thought I had some kind of handle on this stuff. At twenty-three, I know better. It started when quantum blew it all to hell, but thermodynamics, solid-state, or any other framework I might choose would be no better. Welcome to (early) twentieth-century physics. Turns out particles and waves are *the same thing.* Think about it. Pool ball = vibrating guitar string. Relativity and time dilation were a piece of cake by comparison. Go fast and time slows down. Weird, but simple. Now, the impossible is not only possible but inevitable. The field-of-fields, my vision of that cosmic jigsaw puzzle — known in the biz as a big TOE (Theory Of Everything) — is revealed for the pipe dream it always was. Take just one example.

Imagine throwing a tennis ball at a concrete wall. Barring any untoward circumstances — say, a bully stealing the ball or terrorists blowing a hole in the concrete — it will bounce back every time. Throw that ball 10,000 times, and it will still bounce back (so long as it doesn't wear out first). Except now there's tunnelling. So this time, make it a little more particular — because this is real, after all, it's physics — and imagine throwing the tennis ball against a wall at your old elementary school. For me, it's the wall in whose shadow I stood that one time when a janitor threw a golf ball off the roof and the rebound caught me right between the eyes so I had to go to the nurse and miss the rest of recess and my little sister heard yet again that my head was "cracked open," thereby ushering in a rash of early childhood fears and nightmares (hers).

So here's the thing.

If I throw an ordinary tennis ball at that very real wall enough times, sooner or later it's going to pass right on through. Not because it's a magic ball, or because it's actually one of those DIY anarchist handbook ball-bearing-and-match-heads-in-a-tennis-ball grenades. It's just that statistically, if I throw the ball enough times, eventually it's bound to happen. That's tunnelling, and that's quantum. I can build a scanning tunnelling electron microscope and have in fact done so in a third-year lab. Though it's finicky as hell, it works. Analogies to the real, macroscopic world don't work any more — except quantum *is* the real world. *Everything* is made up of atoms, which are made up of "particles" (which aren't really particles *or* waves) that act just like that imaginary tennis ball. And that's just the tip of the electron-cloud.

Later at the party, Bruce catches me on my way out of the bathroom. He says he needs to talk for a minute and leads me to an empty bedroom. Like the rest of the house, the room is a mess. Discarded clothes form a layer of rich humus, revealing only patches of the carpet beneath; glasses, mugs, and full ashtrays cover every available surface. Pinup girls in bikinis and wet T-shirts watch us from dog-eared posters that paper the cracked-plaster walls. I am high enough now that nothing can surprise me. Time is a chain of discrete two-minute contiguous links, nothing more. Later, I may string these links together into some kind of order, but not now. I feel wise for having recognized this. Bruce sits backwards, spraddle-legged on a wooden chair, motions for me to sit on the unmade bed, and offers me a fresh can of beer. I accept.

"There's something I've got to tell you. It's no big deal, but I've got to tell you."

I nod, take a sip of Coors.

"It's a condition of my parole, actually. Anything more than ten hours, and it's pretty much required."

I wait, feeling very Zen about it.

"It was just a paperwork thing, really." Bruce pauses. He seems more pensive than nervous. "See, I had this exporting business, and apparently I messed up some paperwork."

I shake my head in understanding. Bureaucrats are always tools of the Man.

"So I got investigated, and they shut down the business." Now it's Bruce's turn to shake his head. "Turned out the infraction fell under the Criminal Code, and I got convicted. And you know what the worst part is? You can't get a P.Eng. certification for seven years after a criminal conviction. Seven *years*."

Ah. Not failed out, kicked out.

"I mean, it was just a small business, shipping parts. But apparently you need special permissions for firearms parts. And how was I supposed to know where they were going? I mean, it's not like I was shipping direct to Libya or something. What any given buyer did with the stuff after they bought it from me was their business." Bruce sighs. "The judge didn't see it that way, though."

I echo Bruce's sigh, playing for time as I try to think of an appropriate response. I raise my beer, forgetting that Bruce doesn't have one at the moment. "Life goes on," I say, can raised high. "To life." I drink.

"So you're okay with that?"

"Sure, no problem." After all, he's supplying the beer. He's a good guy. It was all just a big misunderstanding. "Shit happens, right?" I feel worldly, rational, magnanimous.

Bruce smiles. "Nothing much fazes you, does it?" He slaps hands on knees, stands, and gestures me over to the window, where he joins me. The glass is single-pane, old, and warped just enough to lend a surreal, wavering edge to the street-lit yard. He points to the shit brown Volkswagen Rabbit in the driveway. "I was thinking," he says, putting a hand on my shoulder and leaving it there. "You see that car? I was going to sell it, but it's not really worth all that much. You want it?"

Wow. A car.

"I mean, it's not in great shape or anything. Needs new brake pads, but it runs okay. And I know a guy who'll certify it for twenty bucks. I figure I could get eight hundred for it, but I'll give it to you for three."

Wow. A car. I don't have one, never have. I'd like to. But . . .

"I dunno," I say. "I'll have to think about it a bit more. When I'm sober."

"Hey, no problem," says Bruce. He slaps me once on the shoulder, breaking contact. "Tell you what. You said you're heading up to Ottawa to visit your girlfriend?" I nod. "Why don't you take the car and see what you think?" Again, I nod. "Consider it payback for all those assignments." My head feels like a yo-yo, bobbing away like that, but I've lost the power of speech and this incessant nodding, it seems, will continue with or without my approval. "Great, so it's settled," Bruce concludes. "That's great."

He leads me back to the bedroom door, opens it, and gestures me through. We return to the party room, where Jeff is painstakingly constructing a pyramid of empty Coors cans.

FOURTH YEAR

At twenty-four, I'm still reeling from the previous
year's schizophrenic collapse of the microscopic
world, and now it looks like the macroscopic universe
will be next to go. It's called *non-linearity, chaos,*
or *complexity.* Complex is a good descriptor, chaos
even better. A highly ordered lunacy is what it is.
Newton's laws hold perfectly well within their limits
(not too big, not too small, not too fast), but even
within those limits the math for the very simplest
of problems — now that we've gotten rid of the
imaginary point-mass pool balls and such — has
become impossible. Not just difficult: impossible. The
notorious three-body problem has *no stable solutions.*
Even rare "special cases" like Lagrange points hide
like needles in an infinite cosmic haystack and
require a whole slew of simplifying assumptions to
make the math work. As for the rest, given starting
positions and momenta, computers can model what
will happen for a while, but sensitivity to initial
conditions means the predictions will eventually
diverge from reality no matter *how* accurately you
measure. Belatedly, I recognize that I could never
reliably calculate the trajectory of a single pool ball
into a single pocket — not even a straight shot. Too
many variables. A jump shot is inconceivable. Pool is
mathematically impossible. And yet, somehow, I find
that I'm much better at it than I was back in first year.

After returning the Rabbit, I will never hear from Bruce again. The possible reasons are endless:

He got the speeding ticket, and he was pissed off. Understandably.

Or, he got the speeding ticket, and when they checked the registration it turned out that Bruce owned the car but hadn't insured it. Bruce is on parole, and driving uninsured is a criminal offence. (True, he wasn't the one driving, but who's going to believe an ex-con who says he lent his car to some guy from a physics class?) Ergo, Bruce is in jail.

Or, Bruce didn't technically "own" the car (just a bit of missing paperwork) and therefore never received the ticket. He simply changed his mind about selling it but didn't have my phone number. (Only now do I realize that we never exchanged phone numbers and relied solely on chance encounters in the physics building for all our communication.)

Or, there was no speeding ticket at all. The apparent photoflash was something else entirely. For the rest, see above.

Maybe Bruce never meant to sell me the car in the first place, but for some obscure reason wanted me to drive it to Ottawa and back. Maybe he used me as a mule. Stranger things can (and surely will) happen. But the true explanation is likely more prosaic. Not until the age of thirty-four does it occur to me that I may have been yet another in Bruce's long string of failed business ventures. In the absence of measurement, Bruce (like Schrödinger's infamous cat) remains both alive and dead, in jail and free, angry and oblivious, duplicitous and naïve. He is a single particle, not an ensemble measurement. Even the existence of the ticket remains undecidable, nothing more (or less) than an expanding probability wave.

THE SMUT STORY (III)

Disabling that economic structure in order to encourage
self-discovery, intelligent relations, individual sexual
freedom, and sexual transcendence on a routine basis
would violate the sanctity of the marketplace, the shrine
within which this cultural, sexual discourse occurs.
The failure or disabling of individual imagination,
so impoverishing to our sexual and emotional lives,
enriches the pornographers.

And that, of course, is why we are not encouraged to
be our own pornographers.

— from Candas Jane Dorsey's "Being One's Own Pornographer"
(as quoted by T.i.o. Boop)

Press Conference
March 14, 2010
Leva Cappucino Bar
Edmonton, AB

Let me be perfectly clear.

The Hermen collective does not know the current where-abouts of Mr. (or Ms.) T. Boop. Any one of us would happily testify under oath that he (or she) was without a doubt one of the most attractive women (or men) we have ever seen. How-ever, try as we might — and trust me, we have tried — we cannot come up with a consistent description. Nor do any of Hermen's members have any knowledge of Ms. (or Mr.) Boop beyond the events of Hermen's Erotica and Pornography Night, now more commonly known as the Mother's Day Affair.

Certain local pundits have suggested that the mere sched-uling of such an event on Mother's Day was in poor taste. The Hermen collective respectfully disagrees. Indeed, we would argue that any attempt, whether implicit or explicit, to repress (or deny) the obvious connections between motherhood and sex is at best misguided. Fuck the virgin-whore dichotomy. However, regardless of any abstract moral(istic) quibbles surrounding the underlying concept and timing of the event itself, the following statement is intended to address some of the more pointed allegations — particularly those of a certain Peter Smith — that have recently resurfaced in several print venues. To wit, Hermen can neither confirm nor deny reports of a "post-reading orgy" following the Mother's Day reading of May 10, 2009.

The collective would have preferred not to respond to these allegations at all, since if you weren't there it's none of your damn business. I mean, seriously. Why do you care? Seems to me you're probably getting off on this too. Nonetheless, given the frequency and persistence of these allegations, as well as the overwhelming public response to said allegations — both censorious and supportive — legal counsel has advised this statement as a necessary compromise.

First, Hermen would like to point out that the lack of credible, mutually corroborating first-hand witnesses to the events in question makes their very existence a matter of dispute. Certain publications have described these alleged events as "improper," "lewd," and even "obscene," and have further argued on this basis that Hermen should be investigated and prosecuted as a "common bawdy house." It is our position that such accusations are not only baseless but quite possibly libellous. And just for the record, Mr. Smith in particular should feel free to go fuck himself.

Nor does Hermen wish to comment on the recent birth of Eva, whose surname will not be repeated here, in deference to her mother's wishes — unlike certain writers working with thinly veiled "anonymous" sources, some of whom we could easily identify were we so inclined. However, unlike *some* people, we hold a healthy respect for the deep vulnerability and resultant expectation of privacy implicit in certain forms of intimate communication, even the privacy of those individuals who seem (apparently) constitutionally incapable of respecting our own. Nor will we speculate on the connections between Eva's birth and the alleged events of that night just over nine months ago. Nonetheless, we both can and do offer our congratulations to Eva's mother on the arrival of her healthy baby girl.

Furthermore, while the Hermen collective can neither confirm nor deny the post-reading events in question, we do affirm that to the best of our knowledge whatever may or may not have happened on the night of the reading was a matter of personal choice on the part of any and all alleged participants. Indeed, none of the published reports to the contrary (and yes, we have read them all) have included even a single first-hand account to corroborate their claims. On this point, even Mr. Smith's morally outraged, symptomatically vague, yet strangely persistent "anonymous" sources have remained uncharacteristically silent.

What Hermen can confirm are the basic events of the reading itself, which were as follows. At seven p.m., Hermen's Erotica and Pornography Night opened its doors to an audience of approximately five, a number which grew closer to twenty by the start of the reading. At eight o'clock, Joel Katelnikoff introduced the theme for the evening, noting that the order of performances would be changed due to the conspicuous absence of the first reader. (At this point, Mr. Katelnikoff may or may not have made certain comments about the absent reader's mother.) Stephanie Bailey then introduced the (formerly) second and third readers, whose pieces were performed without incident and generally well-received.

During the break, an audience member approached Mr. Katelnikoff and offered to fill in for the missing reader with a piece entitled "(The Importance Of) Being One's Own Pornographer." This audience member was, of course, the now-infamous T. Boop. In consultation with the rest of the collective, Mr. Katelnikoff agreed to include Boop's piece as a preferable alternative to cutting the reading short. Mark Woytiuk, in the course of this consultation, further commented that, "If nothing else, she's got a great voice." This statement prompted double-takes from certain group members but passed without further comment.

The performances resumed with the third reader, whose piece was also well-received, after which Ms. Bailey introduced "Mr." T. Boop — again prompting double-takes from several audience members — as a newcomer to Hermen. She also read Boop's supplied introduction, which consisted solely of an epigraph quoted from Candas Jane Dorsey's "Being One's Own

Pornographer." Audience members have universally described Boop as a powerfully attractive person of indeterminate age, average height and build, and nondescript dress. Boop's gender, however, remains unknown, with various audience members recalling the reader as distinctly — and even notably — female, transgendered, androgynous, or male.

What? No, *convenient* is not at all the word I would use.

It's hardly *convenient* for us to have to try to explain any of this. Personally — and I'm sure that in this I speak for everyone who was there — I would much prefer to know who Boop really was. Not to mention, I for one would very much like to see (and especially hear) her again. Now please, if you could just let me finish.

All agree that the piece was structured as a nested second-person narrative, describing an unnamed "you" recounting an explicitly pornographic first-person anecdote to her (or his) unnamed lover. Audience members further reported that their immediate surroundings seemed to "recede" or "fall away" under the influence of Boop's voice, a voice described alternatively as "sonorous," "soft-spoken," "deep," "childlike," "husky," or even "operatic." Myself, I would call it melodious, even musical. Or incantatory, like a spell . . .

But where was I? Ah yes.

In spite of broad agreement regarding the structure and subjective effect of the piece — succinctly described by Hermen organizer Eleni Loutas as "one for the spank bank" — no two members of the audience (or the Hermen collective, for that matter) recall T. Boop's story as depicting the same narrative. Depending on the individual, the story may be recalled as containing explicit scenes of homosexual, transvestite, transgendered, BDSM, incestuous, cross-generational, and even — in some instances — entirely vanilla, heterosexual sex. Thus, in spite of certain passages having been widely (and irresponsibly) reported as "verbatim" reproductions, the precise

contents of Boop's reading, like the gender of the reader her-
(or him-) self, remain unverifiable.

No, I don't *expect* you to believe anything. And frankly,
I don't care. I'm sure you've all heard the expression *you had
to be there?* Well in this case you really did. And you weren't.
If you want to make up a story, feel free. But in that case, please
recognize *and acknowledge* that that's what you're doing.

No, I'm not being facetious. Seriously, have fun with it.
I know we have, and I expect we will continue to do so. But
unlike some, we haven't printed every batshit crazy specula-
tion that came into our heads as fact. And we would thank you
to show the same restraint.

No, I . . .

That isn't what I said.

Look, do you want me to finish or not?

During Boop's performance, certain audience members
saw fit to slam down their glasses, noisily gather their belongings, and pointedly exit the premises. (It should of course
go without saying that none of these early-departing audience members have the slightest idea what may or may
not have happened after the reading. So please bear that
in mind when interviewing your "sources," anonymous or
otherwise.) Nonetheless, in spite of these interruptions, the
piece continued successfully to its conclusion, at which point
Boop referred back to his (or her) bio/epigraph, explicitly
encouraging audience members to become their own pornographers by expanding upon her (or his) story in conversation
amongst themselves.

Seriously? No seriously, how the hell would I know that?

Look, if you want to know what Peter Smith and his so-
called "sources" are on about, you're going to have to ask him
yourself. We would have been happy to talk to him at any point
in this process, but he hasn't contacted us. In fact, we have tried
to contact him repeatedly over the past nine months, but he

hasn't returned any of our calls. He hasn't talked to any of us since . . . Well, let's just say he hasn't consulted us on any of his articles.

Like I said, you'd have to ask him.

And while you're at it, maybe ask him what he was doing that night.

Now please. I'm almost done.

It is the official position of the Hermen collective that any conversations, storytelling, or other interactions which arose and/or continued at this point — whether on the premises or elsewhere — were entirely private and therefore remain beyond the ability (or right) of the Hermen collective to either report or comment upon. Nonetheless, the collective affirms and supports the right of Ms. (or Mr.) Boop to present his (or her) work in whatever form and venue she (or he) may choose. And we encourage him (or her) to continue to do so. Indeed, we would be honoured to have her (or him) perform with us again were he (or she) so inclined.

For although the alleged post-reading events can be neither confirmed nor denied, many of the alleged participants in these alleged activities have (allegedly) described said activities as quite enjoyable indeed. Hermen's official stance on the alleged events themselves, however, can be summarized in two words: "No comment."

MINDREADER

"You ever think about having kids?"

What I say is, "No, not really."

What I mean is, *I've tried to imagine that, but I can't.*

She looks at me — that look — then turns back to the TV.

The World Vision ad ends with a celebrity pitch, replaced by a tampon commercial, a dreamlike image-stream awash in blues, whites, and greens. A blonde woman in English riding gear jumps a white horse over a green hedge. A brunette in a white one-piece bathing suit dives into a kidney-shaped, blue-tiled pool. And so on, closing on a package, white clouds on a blue background. We watch silently, sip our beer from cans. I squeeze her shoulder and smile as the news comes back on, aiming for self-deprecating reassurance. She's focused on the TV, doesn't see the smile, and shrugs off the squeeze with a no-look twitch.

She almost never hears what I mean. But I suppose I can hardly blame her. How many times have I told her, *I can't read your mind. What am I, some kind of goddamn psychic?* Course, most times that's me trying to cover my own fuck up. It generally works, too, puts her on the defensive, as intended. But it isn't always true.

Like when she says, "Do you like this outfit?"

What she really means is, *Do you like me?*

Like? Christ, I love her. What do I care about clothes?

I always look, though, make a show of eyeing her up and down. She's getting older, sure. But still. Her face is well-preserved, smooth in a fighting-off-the-wrinkles kind of way. It's the eyes that give her away, that tired look she gets when she thinks no one's watching. The look disappears when she smiles, so I try to make her do that as often as I can, which is less often than I'd like. She's got the sculpted calves of a career-waitress, carved by hours of standing in those damn heels. (Good for tips, she says. I say the fuckers oughta tip her for the privilege of sharing the same room, heels or no.) Incredible figure, all things considered. But she complains about her body. Standing in front of the mirror, she flips a hand back and forth at the wrist, arm held out perpendicular to her body, and points to the offending tricep-wobble.

"It didn't used to *do* that," she says.

I wrap my arms around her waist from behind, kiss her neck and whisper in her ear. The usual sweet nothings, content irrelevant. As I do this, I watch the slouching, balding guy in the mirror, some dirty old man pawing this gorgeous woman who's totally out of his league. If I told her I like it best when she bums around the apartment in old sweats, it might be the gods-honest truth, but she'd never believe it.

Not that I'm entirely oblivious. On someone else, say some woman I didn't know, I might notice the clothes. I might say, "Yeah, that's pretty hot." And I'd know I was referring to the whole performance, the look, the clothes, the way she carried herself. Course I wouldn't *say* it. And besides, who cares? I don't know that woman.

But here and now, in our own apartment, seriously, fuck the outfit. Outfits are for strangers. So when she asks, I say (truth- fully), "Looks good to me," and shrug. She thinks that means I don't care. Which is both true and untrue, but not in the ways that she thinks.

Another time, she says, "Do you love me?"

Translation: *I'm afraid that you don't. Prove it.*

How do you prove love?

Mornings, wrapped up tight in that beige-bland, form-fitting uniform, she leaves for work while I'm still sitting at the kitchen table. Hesitating in the open doorway, she lets in a gust of cold air. I'm in my bathrobe, face still puffy from sleep, coffee in one hand, smoke in the other, newspaper open on the table in front of me. I pretend I don't see her looking, circle an ad in the paper. Projecting for all I'm worth. *See? Not even awake yet, but I'm already looking.* And she stands there giving me this look. Not that look. A different one.

This one makes me think of an empty beach tucked away at the end of a series of low-maintenance trails. Algonquin Park, the two of us lying on her sarong, sweat-slicked and drying in the sun. She holds me sprawled across her chest like a slob- bery drunk as I doze in self-absorbed, post-coital stupor. A bee hovers by my face, and she waves it off. "You leave him alone," she says. "He's mine." I pretend I'm sleeping.

But that was a long time ago, and the camping gear was borrowed. More likely, when she looks at me like that, half- way out the door on her way to work for the rent that I rarely help to pay, she's thinking, *I can do better than this.*

What she says is, "Bye, hon. See you tonight."

59

I imagine her on the bus downtown, wedging herself into a seat between familiar-faced strangers. (You get to recognize them, same ones every day.) She looks at the ads, ignores the rest of the poor slobs stuck on early-morning public transit, and they ignore her back. A sort of solidarity. At home, I finish my coffee and go back to bed. Maybe make a few phone calls, read a book, watch TV. I've got nowhere to be. By the time I've showered and dressed, she'll be on her first break.

That's most days.

Other times, I go to that lot downtown, the one on Charles. Pick-up time's six a.m. Hard to wake up for that. But always, eventually, it's easier to drag my sorry ass down there than sit around the apartment waiting for the phone to ring. So I set the alarm, get up while she's still sleeping, and take the bus downtown in the dark. I did it this morning.

We stand in a huddled crowd, maybe thirty of us, hands wrapped around steaming styrofoam cups. Slanting light punches through gaps between buildings, crowbars into squinting, slitted eyes. We blink like groundhogs too stunned and groggy to look for a shadow. The van pulls up and a young guy gets out, points.

"You and you . . . you three . . . and you two over there. Let's go."

We climb in the back, perch on slippery bales of flyers or hunker down on the plywood flooring. They've ripped out the insides to make more space, so we sit in facing rows, leaning back against the van's exposed metal guts. On the road to Hamilton, the one with the clipboard collects names and social insurance numbers. Beside me is Clark Kent, social insurance number 519 911 411. Mine is 382 596 888: *FUCK YOUUU* on your touch-tone dial. Across from me sit Kurt Russell and

Kris Kristofferson. The guy with the clipboard just writes it all down, doesn't even crack a smile for Huey, Dewey, and Louie McDuck. He's not stupid, but it's minimum wage paid in cash at the end of the day. What kind of asshole would make you report a lousy forty bucks? Not this kind of asshole. I wonder what he makes in a day.

They drop us off, assign our territory in five-block chunks, give us each a stack of flyers and a canvas bag. We head out one at a time, a ragged troop of aging paperboys. You get to your block and start delivering. The flyers weigh about fifty pounds. Feels light at first, but the canvas strap doesn't have any padding, and by the time you're halfway down the block it starts to chafe. At five blocks, you forget the chafing as the strap sinks into muscle. Now your neck hurts, and you might experiment with different ways of slinging the bag. Never works, though, and by ten blocks you get used to it. The pain doesn't fade. Just becomes a part of the fabric of the day.

Every now and then some smartass dumps his load in a ravine or a ditch and buggers off to the bar till pickup. They do random checks for that, though, so most of us deliver. Most houses are empty, but every now and then you catch someone at home. Or they catch you. A youngish woman in a skirt and blouse, attractive in a bland Sears Catalogue kind of way, might abruptly open the door just as you're about to leave.

"Look, we don't want these things." She waves a rolled-up sheaf of flyers for emphasis. Maybe she throws them on the ground. "We get these things every week, and we never look at them." You might shrug. There's no point in explaining that you've never been here before and probably never will be again. You bend down to pick up the flyers, and she keeps talking. "We used to have a wood stove but we never use it any more and these things just keep piling up. We don't need the flyers, okay?" She's having a bad day. *First the plumber, then the phone guy, and now this.*

Lot of guys might get mouthy at this point. I tell her to put up a sign. We're supposed to watch for no-flyer signs, but sometimes if I'm hungover I ignore them. My big act of rebellion. I imagine myself a Ché Guevara of the 'burbs, stealthily bludgeoning self-satisfied mortgage holders into submission, one flyer at a time.

Another woman, older and wearing a bathrobe over pyjamas, might butt out her cigarette in an overflowing ashtray as you walk up the drive. ("The way I see it, that's my job," one of these women once told me. "To fill up this ashtray.") She's been waiting, and she's so glad you brought her flyer. Last week, she didn't get it and there was this special over at Knob Hill Farms and she didn't hear about it and had to pay full price for potatoes when she could have got them cheap if she'd just got her flyer. It's a half-hearted sort of complaining. She's not blind (yet). You're pushing forty and delivering junk mail for a living. She can understand that.

The complaints are more an excuse for conversation, like the lumbago flare-up or Kids Today. You're not supposed to do anything about it. Just listen, hand over the flyer, mumble something sympathetic, and move on. By the time you're two doors down, you've forgotten her face. Only the ashtray, pyjamas, and bathrobe remain.

A cream-painted steel door swings open, and I fall forward, a handful of flyers scattering across linoleum as I catch myself on hands and knees. Now, instead of a mail slot, I'm looking at a pair of feminine feet, bright red toenails. My eyes rise, climbing a cool waterfall of skin, smooth calves topped by thighs that flash bare for a provocative inch or two before disappearing behind sheer fabric.

Eyes on the floor, I scramble to gather up the flyers, shoving them back into the bag, which keeps falling open to spill them back out again. Shit. Slow down. Kneel and balance the bag against my thigh, try again. By the time I've got them all back in, she still hasn't said a word. I look up again to find the woman attached to those legs squinting down at me like she's trying to figure something out. I just kneel there like an idiot, staring.

"Well, speak of the devil," she says. "That *is* you, isn't it? Jimmy Winters?"

I stand slowly, brushing my pants. This particular Sears Catalogue woman wears a red silk kimono, lingerie section. Nice outfit. She holds a drink in one hand and waves me in with the other, sloshing a little in the process.

"Come on in and have a drink. I'm celebrating."

Feels like I've stumbled into a bad '70s porn. The wah-wah guitars should be kicking in any second now. I flub my line.

"I don't know. I'm kind of on a —"

"You don't remember me, do you?" She squints and pokes an unsteady finger at my chest. "I remember *you* though. Now get your ass in here and have a drink. It's a special occasion. Once in a lifetime, maybe. They've got to give you breaks, right?"

Well no, actually, they don't.

"Well, I guess I could . . ."

That brief hesitation is all the encouragement she needs to grab my arm and propel me into the living room.

"Still working out, I see." She gives my bicep a firm squeeze. "Just toss that wherever," she says, indicating the flyers. "Sit down, make yourself at home. *Mi casa* and all that." Then she disappears through a door to what must be the kitchen.

I heave the bag over my head, set it by the end of the couch and look around. The place is huge, hardwood trim everywhere, spotless white carpet, a gas fireplace. Wedding photos in wrought iron frames on the mantle. The whole room is done up in creams and whites. I feel like I'm getting it dirty just by looking.

A call from the kitchen: "I've got scotch or vodka. You like scotch?"

"Uh, scotch is fine," I call back. "What's the occasion?"

"Rocks or neat?" she says, emerging with a bottle in one hand, two large glasses in the other. A single ice cube rattles in one of the glasses.

"Rocks, I guess."

"Sit down, take a load off," she says, handing me the glass with the lonely ice cube and pushing me onto the couch. She sits beside me, curls her feet up beneath her, refills her own glass, and leans forward to pour mine. The kimono doesn't quite close at the neck, and she isn't wearing anything underneath. She takes her time pouring, filling the glass halfway to the top. I focus on the ice cube.

"Cheers," I say, raising my drink.

"To unexpected visitors," she says, raising hers. "Sláinte!" Clinking glasses, she overshoots and again spills a bit, then downs a hefty gulp. I take a small sip. Carefully. She leans back, closes one eye for focus, and looks me up and down. "You really don't remember me, do you?"

"Well, I . . ."

"No, it's okay. Why should you remember? Christy Albertson." A formal handshake. "I was in grade nine when you were in grade twelve. You know how it is . . ." She closes her eyes, tilts her head back. Her long neck is punctuated by small divots at each end: that space between jaw and ear above; below, a tiny hollow just over the collarbone. "Older kids, they seem larger than life at that age."

"So, uh, what's the occasion?" *Jesus. Little Christy Albertson, all grown up.*

She opens her eyes, takes a small plastic baton from the kimono's breast pocket, and waves it in the air like a checkered flag.

"I'm pregnant. Just checked."

"Congratulations."

"Yeah, turns out good ol' Marty had it in him after all. Who'da thunk? Been trying for years now. Always knew it was a long shot. So to speak." Drop to a drunken stage-whisper. "Marty has a *very* low sperm count." Back to normal volume. "Looks like he beat the odds this time, though!" She raises her glass. "Here's to Marty's Miracle! He'll be so proud."

"You haven't told him yet?"

"Nope. You're the first to know. He's in Illinois on business, calls every night. Such a sweet man, my Marty. So devoted."

"Sounds like you've got it made. Great guy and a little one on the way. Great place too."

"You like it?" She waves a hand to the room. "Picked it all out myself, and God knows Martin can afford it. I love this place, really I do. I'm very lucky." She examines the room, then looks at me and leans forward. "You know what?" She exhales, and the smell of alcohol intensifies as the imaginary wah-wah guitars grow more insistent. The kimono opens a little more, and this time I see all the way down. Nice view. Hard to believe she's only three years younger than me. Good living, I suppose.

"You know, I had a crush on you back then." She leans even farther forward and places a hand on each of my forearms. I tense reflexively under the weight and spill half my drink on that spotless white carpet.

"Shit!" I jump up off the couch. "Shit, I'm sorry." That's going to stain, and she . . . And Martin . . . "You got a cloth or something?" I head to the kitchen — which is as spotless as the living room — grab a roll of paper towels, rush back out front. And stop. Christy sits on the floor by the puddle of scotch, laughing so hard the tears are rolling down her cheeks to drip off her chin. I hand her a paper towel, and she dabs at her eyes.

"Thanks," she says, still giggling. "You know, you haven't changed a bit."

"Look . . . I, uh . . . I better . . ."

Christy's hands flutter against her chest as she struggles to speak through resurgent laughter. "Yes, you . . . Good to . . ." Unable to complete a sentence, she nods and mimes her assent with a vaguely convulsive gesture, halfway between a wave and a shooing-off. I pick up the canvas sack and head for the front door. Miraculously, not a drop of scotch has landed on either my clothes or the flyers.

Of course I knew about the crush. Everybody did. She made it hard to miss, the way she'd sit in the weight room and chatter aimlessly about nothing while I did curls, triceps, leg-extensions, or whatever. The guys bugged me about it, half-mocking, half-debating the proper course of action. Bill Hereford succinctly summed up the go-for-it faction's opinion. "Old enough to bleed, old enough to breed," he said. Oh, and I thought about it. Christy didn't look fourteen then any more than she looks thirty-five now. She was a little hottie. Still is.

And as I leave, quietly closing the door and checking myself for spillage, that same little hottie is slowly pouring the contents of a nearly full bottle of very expensive scotch onto her (formerly) spotless white carpet. And laughing. I cut across the lawn to the next house, adjust the strap on my shoulder. As always, it makes no difference.

In the van on the way home, the guy with the clipboard hands out cash. Travel time's only paid one way, so our hours were done the moment we climbed in. He calls out the names recorded on his sheet, and one by one, we raise our hands, take our money, double-count it just to be sure. Everybody's real quiet as clipboard guy peels fives, tens, and twenties off the thick wad of bills, and this time no one laughs at Huey, Dewey, and Louie McDuck. Halfway back to Kitchener, the mood shifts and some of the guys get to talking. Kris Kristofferson and Clark Kent say they're heading to the Mayfair soon as we get back. The young guy with the forgettable name stays quiet. Never speaks unless he's spoken to, and even then his answers are short and vague. He looks seventeen, eighteen at most. He won't be doing this for long. I don't do it much myself, but it's been off and on ten years now. Kris Kristofferson is going on about how wrecked he's going to get at the Mayfair. Among other things.

"Gonna get *laid* tonight, boys," he says.

"Yeah, you and the Palm twins, I hear you got a thing going," says Clark Kent. Laughter all around, and Kent looks pleased with himself. Kristofferson turns to the young guy, leaning forward. A chin-jerk in Kent's direction.

"Him, he's just jealous. You should've seen the one I got last week. Legs on up to forever, sweet little thing comes straight up to me and you know what she does?" Kristofferson pauses and Kent rolls his eyes. "*She* offers to buy *me* a drink."

The kid listens politely.

"And I'm thinking there's gotta be a catch, like maybe she's a hooker or one of them she-male types. Like in *The Crying Game*, you know? Man, that's one fucked up flick." He's got a hand on the kid's shoulder now, and the kid looks about ready to sink through the floor with embarrassment. "And I don't want none of that, so I reach right up there under that tiny little skirt and give a *real* good squeeze. And you know what she does?" No response. "She says 'Oh, *baby*, that feels *gooood*.' And now I'm really shitting cause there's nothing down there that ain't supposed to be. Not to mention she's dripping like a leaky faucet, if you know what I mean."

Poor kid looks terrified.

"Turns out her old man works nights, and boy did we have us a hell of a time back at their place." He grins and slaps the kid on the back. "One hell of a time. Say, you're not a bad-looking guy. You ought to come with us." The kid looks like he wants to puke, mumbles something about ID.

"ID? Fuck ID. You don't need ID at the Mayfair! I'll vouch for you."

Nobody calls Kristofferson on the story, and some of the guys were there, so part of it might even be true. Kristofferson's got that same tanned look as the rest of us. (More like a hide than a beach-bunny.) Put a cowboy hat on him and he might look like some kind of good ol' boy, tanned from a hard day of range-riding instead of pounding suburban pavement. It might work. Stranger things have happened.

I'm home for twenty minutes or so before she walks through the door. Just long enough to get the beer in the fridge and let it chill a bit. I hand her the leftover cash and the first can of the first six-pack.

"Thanks, hon," she says. "That's just what I needed." Then she kicks off her heels and flops onto the couch. No translation required.

I sit beside her as she watches the news. Imagine getting up to turn down the volume at the next commercial. Coming back to the couch and going down on one knee. She might look at me, eyes bright and shining. Maybe a tear runs down her cheek. She can't stop smiling, and I speak real low: "Laurie, I been thinking . . ."

I could do that. In my head, I've already done it eight, nine, maybe a dozen times.

A Volkswagen ad comes on. I get up and look at her. She

doesn't notice me looking. She's lost in those mountain vistas, that corner-hugging suspension. I grab two more cold beers from the fridge, pop them open, and hand one to her.

"Thanks, hon," she says, takes a sip, and sets the can on the coffee table. Then leans back into the arc of my waiting arm, lays a hand on my chest, and nuzzles the top of her head into the hollow under my chin.

JUNK MAIL

OUTSIDE ADDRESS:

So here's this kid, grinning fit to bust. He's barely cracked the shell of his third decade, emerging fresh into adulthood like a new-hatched chick, shiny and slick with birth effluvia. He's twenty-two at most. And here's me, at the end of my driveway, nearing the end of that same third decade, not yet fully awake on my way to work, wishing I could crawl back into the shell and seal it up forever behind me. I walk to work because, although it's only three blocks, it gives me a chance to prepare myself for the plunge into shiny-happy office land. The whole way there, I practice my plastic smile.

Grin-boy wears jeans, a cotton jacket, and a T-shirt. He's got sideburns, lamb-chops like I used to have, scruffy hair just a bit too long. Hasn't shaved for a few days. He smiles right at me, like I've told this great joke or maybe the whole world's a joke, and a good one at that. He lurches along in short, shuffling strides, but there's a spring to his step. Every fourth or fifth step he gives a joyous little hop. There is no hate like early-morning hate, sudden, pure, and visceral.

71

"I'm a squash," he says to me, and giggles as he passes.

DELIVERY

Brian McKierney received a letter this morning. He hasn't read it yet, hasn't even noticed it, just stuffed it into his briefcase along with the usual wad of envelopes. Brian is more or less indistinguishable from any other person walking down the street, averts his eyes in the proper North American way, slips smoothly, invisibly through his daily routines. Like many, he is not entirely content with his position in life but possesses a vague conviction that it will continue to improve. (He would, however, find himself hard put to identify any improvements beyond an incrementally rising income.) He could be almost anyone: your co-worker, your boss, your lover, your sister's first boyfriend who was an asshole to her but other than that seemed like an okay guy. He is not you. Or at least, the odds are astronomically against it.

INSIDE ADDRESS:

I order a Firkin A. The Firkin Fox brew pub (slogan: "Give me a Firkin beer") buzzes with straight-from-work chatter. Standing at the bar, I light a cigarette, snag an ashtray. At the table directly behind me, someone coughs conspicuously. At another table farther down, my co-workers discuss *The Simpsons*. Anton insists it's not what it used to be, prompting a spate of quotes and reminiscences. *You know that one where Bart calls Moe's and . . . ? Now that one was great.* The guy on the stool next to me wears plaid pants, an anarchy T-shirt, a toque. Fresh piercings glint at his eyebrow and septum, nestled deep in angry red swollen flesh. I feel vaguely middle-aged next to him, though I'm not.

Yet. He turns to me.

"I'm not a squash today," he says. "Buy me a drink."

Funny. I hadn't recognized him. Maybe it's that he's not smiling. Maybe it's the toque.

"What you drinking?"

"Rye and ginger. Beer puts me to sleep."

My Firkin A arrives, dark and cloudy, tastes like smoke. I order a rye and ginger, pull up a stool, and sit.

"So you're not a squash."

"Nope."

"But sometimes you say you are."

"Sometimes I am," he corrects me. "Not so's you'd see it — more of an under-the-skin thing — but when I say it, it's the truth. It comes and goes."

"That's crazy."

"Yup. Absolutely insane. Clinically diagnosed. Schizophrenic, in fact."

His drink arrives. I pay for it.

"How'd you get to be like that?"

"Beats me," he says. He holds up his glass. A toast: "No laboratory findings have been identified that are diagnostic of schizophrenia!" He gulps half his drink at one go, bangs the glass decisively down on the counter, then shrugs. "Just one of those things. Far as I can tell, it's a process of elimination. If you have bizarre delusions — which are completely different from the non-bizarre kind — then you're schizophrenic. If you're not doing acid or something. That's the elimination part. My psychiatrist could tell you all the technical details."

He can't afford a rye and ginger but he can afford the hundred-plus dollars an hour for a shrink? My benefits are good, but they only cover psychologists, and the waiting lists for psychiatrists are ridiculous, six to eight months minimum. Unless you're on welfare.

"You've got a psychiatrist?"

"Nope," he says. "Hey, you got an extra smoke?"

I pass him a cigarette and lighter. Back at the table, they've progressed from *The Simpsons* to *Survivor*. Anton predicts the gay guy will be next to go, and everyone agrees. The guy's so annoyingly paranoid, thinks everybody hates him because he's gay. Truth is, no one likes him because he insists everyone hates him. It's a self-fulfilling prophecy, a feedback loop, a strange attractor. Anton's into chaos theory at the moment. I'd think strange repeller would be more appropriate, but — thankfully — I'm not a part of that conversation.

"So, your nonexistent psychiatrist diagnosed you as schizophrenic. Because you think you're a squash. Sometimes." I look around to see if anyone's catching this, but the bartender's riveted to the Olympic curling coverage. Captivating stuff. The guy at the other end of the bar stares off into space, eyes unfocused. He could be listening. I don't have to turn around to know the people at the table behind me have moved.

"Former psychiatrist. The guy had me strung out on neuroleptics: haloperidol, chlorpromazine, olanzapine, fluphenazine. Went back to the haloperidol injections when I got careless with the pills. They all worked, too. When I was on them, I never once turned squash." He stops, makes this sudden face: cheeks pulled back in what might be a smile if his eyebrows didn't scrunch down low like that. And if he wasn't making that chewing motion at the same time. He looks away, and when he looks back his face has returned to normal.

"So that's good, right?"

"Depends on how you look at it. I never got confused, but I never got happy either. Never got sad or horny or scared or angry or excited or bored. Nothing."

"That sucks," I say.

"You'd think so, wouldn't you?" He makes another face: eyebrows raised, eyes wide, lips puckered. Then drops it and continues. "Didn't bother me at the time, though. Nothing did, not the drowsiness or the blurred vision or the shakiness. Not even the muscle spasms. Except I met this guy in the waiting room."

"Yeah?"

"Yeah. This one guy, he's twitchy like all of us, but he stands out 'cause he's got this energy. The rest of us are all good little zombies. Anyway, the guy walks straight up to me and delivers this massive lecture right out of the blue, all about how neuroleptics cause permanent brain-damage, how people like us don't get better in this country. Then he shows me some photocopies from the DSM-IV —"

"The what?"

"DSM-IV — it's, like, the psychiatrist's bible. Anyway, he shows me where it says living in a developed country is a 'strong predictor for poor long-term outcomes.' 'Now why's that?' I ask, 'cause I don't see the connection. 'The drugs, you basket-case!' he says. He rolls his eyes like maybe I'm a little dense. 'In this country, we can afford the latest, state-of-the-art pharmaceuticals. In developing countries they can't. So they don't use them. Funny thing is, they get better and we don't.' So I think about that for a bit and figure what the hell. I'll try anything once. So I walk out of there and never go back." He downs the rest of his drink. "Good thing I gave him a fake name."

"The guy?"

"Him too, but I was talking about the psychiatrist."

"Why?"

"What are you, the only guy in the western hemisphere who hasn't heard the term *paranoid schizophrenic*?" He picks up his glass, sees it's empty, and sets it back down. "Another?"

Sure, what the hell. I order another round while my temporarily-hominid companion makes a series of faces.

"Why do you do that?"

"Do what?"

"Make those faces."

"Oh, that. Tardive dyskinesia. It's a side-effect."

"Of the schizophrenia?"

"Of the meds."

"But you're off the meds."

"Doesn't matter. It's permanent."

I take out two more cigarettes, light one, hand him the other along with the lighter. We smoke in silence until our drinks arrive.

"Seriously, though, the fake name was a good thing. I was on community treatment order, so they could pick me up if they thought I was avoiding medication. Buddy in the waiting room said he knew ways around that, but the fake name made it easier. So here I am . . ." He turns and spreads his arms, taking in the whole bar, booths, stools, after-work crowd, two televisions, glowing beer signs, fake wood trim, half-hearted pub décor, the taps. ". . . a roam-as-I-choose kinda guy, clean and drug-free. With a few notable exceptions." A lopsided half-grin as he raises his glass. "Totally average guy, that's me, 'cept sometimes, I'm a squash."

"Always a squash?"

"Usually. I was an eagle once." He pauses and smiles, eyes focusing on something I can't see. "Now *that* was fun. You ever heard an eagle's cry? Scared the shit out of some people in the park. It's how they picked me up in the first place." He shakes his head abruptly, finishes his drink, and sticks out his hand. "I'm Sebastian," he says. Not his real name. We shake hands.

"Nice to meet you, Sebastian. I'm Jason." Not my real name either. I stand. "Maybe I'll see you around."

"Yeah, see you."

Sebastian turns to watch the curling. I walk over to the table, join my co-workers.

"You know that guy?" Stephen asks. Stephen's in sales support. Not too bright, but he's got a good track record. People like to buy from someone who makes them look smart by comparison. I doubt Stephen realizes this.

"Met him once before. Interesting guy. He thinks he's a squash. Sometimes."

Stephen raises an eyebrow, then turns back to the conversation in progress. I get that reaction sometimes. They're discussing the war.

"Face it," says Jolene (marketing), "the Canadian military's underfunded. If we want the Americans to take us seriously, we're going to have to invest some serious cash."

"We don't have the tax-base for that," says Eric (developer). "What we need is just what we've got — an elite, highly specialized fighting force. Forget the big guns. Bigger is not necessarily better."

"Is that what your girlfriend's telling you?" Stephen can't resist. "Dude, forget the military, you're in some serious trouble."

And so on.

I, for one, am not worried about the international street-cred of our armed forces or the threat of terrorism. I do not live in New York, do not work at the World Trade Centre, the White House, or the Pentagon. I do not live in Afghanistan, Iraq, Palestine, or Israel. I am not now, nor have I ever been, a squash.

DELIVERY

Brian works as a personal service representative for Great Modern Life Insurance where, as per his job description, he liaises by phone with claimants, requests additional information as necessary, and updates the relevant files. The term *adjuster* makes him wince. His job is nothing like the Egoyan film, and he resents the association. Like *The Adjuster*'s title character, Brian helps clients negotiate the bureaucracy required to verify their claims. But the resemblance ends there. For starters, Brian never meets his clients in person, would never know if he passed one by on the street. Great Modern never sends personal service representatives into the field, though they do hire freelance investigators to verify the more statistically questionable claims. Just in case. Most people may be honest, but statistics don't lie.

Brian's job is limited to answering questions, typing up forms, and making sure each claim is thoroughly documented. Even short-term disability claims are relatively straightforward, operating on a simple algorithm. Statistics show that any client not returning to work within six months is unlikely ever to do so. However, clients receiving no payment for five months are 90% more likely to return to work before that window ends. Brian doesn't know exactly how this information was gathered — that's what actuaries are for — but he trusts the information is accurate and follows standard procedure. And once all procedures have been followed, all documentation duly verified and filed, Brian signs off on the cheques.

If asked in a social setting, Brian would characterize his job as helping people at a time when they need it most. If asked by his superiors, he would characterize it as a watchdog process, a constant vigilance against fraudulent claims. If confronted, he would see no contradiction between these two characterizations. And yet, each time he re-watches that film, *The Adjuster*'s home-destroying fire at the end evokes a strangely cathartic rush, and he finds himself compulsively imagining how that might feel. To have everything vanish in a sudden burst of flame and smoke. The heat on his face as he watched it all burn.

ATTENTION LINE:

A blinding, silent flash. A sharp *CRACK!* shakes the building, followed by rolling, rumbling aftershocks. Fluorescent lights flicker and for a moment UPS-powered computer monitors are the only light in the room.

"That was close," I say. It's been storming like this all morning.

"I almost got struck by lightning on the way in to work, eh?" says Jacky. "This huge flash, like, ten feet in front of my car, right in the middle of the road. I could've been killed."

We share a cubicle, Jacky and I. Sometimes I wonder about her.

"You're so full of shit."

"No, really. Right there in front of me. I could smell the ozone."

"How would you know what ozone smells like?"

"It smells hot, like burnt air."

"Burnt air?"

"You know, sometimes people get struck by lightning and walk away a genius."

"Yeah, in comic books, maybe. In real life, they walk away dead. Or an idiot."

"It's a fine line between genius and idiot."

No it's not. The line between genius and idiocy is a big fat freaking eight-lane highway, and if you can't see that, then we know which side of the line you're on, now don't we? Or we would, if idiots didn't blend in so well. There is, after all, a certain safety in numbers. That's what I want to say. Instead, I stare at her, trying to figure out what she means.

"You're bluescreening," says Jacky.

RETURN ADDRESS:

I go straight to the Firkin after work.

I'm by myself, which is fine. There's hardly anyone here today: a long narrow room, a row of vacant booths across from the bar. It looks different when it's empty. Shabbier. An intermittent clicking of pool balls drifts down the stairs, punctuated by the occasional exclamation: *Nice shot!* or *You bastard!*

Down here, a textured silence: the dull clink of the bartender shelving glasses, low mumble of the sports report, liquid hum and shush of the glass-washer. No music. The guys at the far end of the bar don't speak, look like they've been here all day. They watch TV and I watch them.

I am so sick of bluescreens. They tell me it's a good thing, a flat-out crash like that, means I'm doing good work, finding all the bugs before our clients get a crack at it. And I've got this knack. I can crash any program and not just the stuff I'm supposed to be testing either. Sometimes I think it's just me and machines or — more specifically — me and electricity. I walk under streetlights: they go out. I assemble my new computer: a great blue flash arcs from the connector cord to the box. Could've killed me, but it didn't. Lucky me.

I pick up my glass, find it's empty, and order another. Ask the bartender about Sebastian, but she says she doesn't know him. Two more beer, seven cigarettes, and innumerable musings later, I pay up and leave. Sebastian doesn't show.

DELIVERY

The lack of a stamp makes him think *junk mail*, but he always opens everything. Just in case. If it's important, it goes into a file. Anything else, he shreds to remove all identifying information. If he can't immediately tell one way or another, he reads it. Carefully. At 6:23 p.m., Brian lays the letter out on the kitchen table, on top of the Publishers Clearing House Sweepstakes ("You may have already won!") and next to the unopened credit card bill. Below the handwritten salutation, the text switches to typescript:

We don't know you. Not personally. But We
do believe certain things. Although you
are most certainly a cog in the machine,
We believe you are also more than that.
More than the sum of your job description
("personal service representative"), employee
number (111116111), most recent income tax
return (file #00-42-58689), middle names
("Andrew Alexander"), age demographic
(25-34), or any other information easily
gleaned from your files. The question is,
do you? Don't worry. You don't have to decide
right away. Allow us to explain . . .

As Brian reads on, he's alarmed at first, then increasingly confused. It's more of a narrative than a pitch. A testimonial? Except there's no product. It could be a joke, but those lists, the middle names he never uses, and the sheer length of the thing — which runs on for several pages — all seem too elaborate for that.

He reads the letter. Or story. Or whatever it is. Then he reads it again.

ON-ARRIVAL NOTATION
(PERSONAL AND CONFIDENTIAL):

"You look at number 4852 yet?"

I minimize Outlook and spin around in my ergonomic swivel chair. I hate it when she does that. Jacky always walks right up behind me before she speaks. How long has she been standing there? I think she likes watching me jump.

"What's the matter?" She smirks. "Afraid we might see your dirty pictures?"

"4852. That's the sub-pixel reverse roll?"

"Yeah, that's it. I ran your sample code, but I didn't see it."

I set it up and show her how it looks on my machine, which is slower than hers. She watches, nods, goes back to her chair to write the report, and smiles. Always, that smile.

Fucking panopticon open-bloody-concept offices. Never should have set up my home email to forward to work. They can read those, you know. No such thing as privacy rights on company time, company servers.

Two weeks ago, a summer student got fired for having "illegal material" on his computer. Buzz is, it was porn and he showed it to one of the women he worked with. Not too bright. One week ago, Stephen showed me his e-porn collection. He's got the corner cubicle, keeps the monitor facing away from the entrance. Two days ago, this friend of mine — makes more money than I do teaching English in Japan with a bloody general arts degree, haven't talked to him in over a year — emails me porn halfway around the world because he thinks it's funny. This huge popup: a naked Asian woman with absurdly large breasts. She hangs frontside-down, feet and hands tied behind her back to this huge iron hook at the end of a thick, heavy-linked chain. In midair, about two feet off the ground, she sucks cock. The picture's cropped so there's no guy, just a big cock. Buddy in Japan called it "hook." Ha ha.

Too late, I turned off the email forwarding and deleted the message. But the file was on the server for hours before I saw it, probably archived to backup, and there's not a goddamn thing I can do about that. Fine line my could've-got-fired ass.

DELIVERY

At 3:49 in the morning, Brian sets down the letter. The faux-leather couch creaks as he leans back and closes his eyes.

A long, slow breath, and he sits back up, rubs his eyes, looks around the room. Graduation portraits of friends and exes, family photos, and a few framed movie posters plaster the walls. Wooden knick-knacks and memorabilia from his sister's travels clutter every available surface. The picture from her wedding looks like a fairy tale, her on a white horse, Brian's brother-in-law standing in front, all three of them blazing white against a background of glowing green: grass, willows, rushes by the pond-bank in the foreground. Even the water is slick and green with algae. This is familiar, utterly normal. This is home.

And yet, everything seems strange.

The light from the reading lamp slants upwards, casting unlikely, inverted shadows. And though he remembers each quick *snap!* of the flash (spots slowly clearing as his vision returned), these pictures seem to show someone else's life, a perfect identical twin with perfect identical memories. Likewise, the furniture — this easy chair, this couch, CD library, tuner, DVD player, twenty-eight inch TV, bookshelves, grey and red and blue spines jabbering nonsensical titles, the leatherbound copy of *Ulysses* never opened but given a place of pride on the top shelf — all purchased by someone else, someone he knows all about but has never met.

Just for a moment, he is free.

IN REPLY TO:

When I get in, I see why the bartender couldn't place Sebastian from my description. He might as well have been wearing a uniform. It's Friday night at the Firkin, standing room only, and these kids have got so much metal stuck in them in so many different ways they remind me of cyborgs. They're closer than you think. Not off in some distant sci-fi future but right now. Myoelectric prosthetics, pacemakers, neural nets, artificial hearts, eyes, kidneys, muscles, skin — utterly innocuous and virtually invisible, they're already here.

The band's called suv Smashup, standard guitar-bass-drums trio, but not bad. I'd call it funk, but it's probably got some special name — Anton, alternative-pop-culture boy, would know for sure. The lead singer-guitarist is a bit pompous, but that's his job. Look at Peter Gabriel, surrounded by all the "serious" musicians of Genesis. Someone taps my shoulder.

"Sebastian! I've been looking for you."

"Yeah, I heard," he says. "Don't do that, okay?"

"All right."

I think of the car parked out in front of my place when I took my time off. Whenever I went out, there'd be that guy in the car. Sometimes he'd be drinking coffee. Other times he'd be on his cell phone, reading, or writing in a little spiral-bound notebook. But always the same guy, the same car. Not particularly subtle, but then I suppose it wasn't meant to be. I figure he worked for the insurance company. They wanted my medical records too, full chart. I would've done it, but the violation of confidentiality put my doctor on edge, and he recommended against it. So I checked the company out, found this one website. Seems at least one guy's family is suing — they say Great Modern Life drove him to suicide by refusing to pay his long-term disability coverage. The company knew he was suicidal, of course: they had the file. But Great Modern's psychiatrists said he was faking. Guess he showed them.

And that's not even the best part. Turns out there are no laws about distributing that kind of information once you give it to them. I checked that too. These companies can do whatever they want with it, put it in their database, share it around, never have to tell you a damn thing. As long as it's a "reasonable" part of their business model, whatever that means. Course, if you don't give out, they don't pay out. Or just put off payment as long as possible, a rigged game of financial chicken, see who flinches first. It's all perfectly legal, innocent even. Everyone's just doing their job, keeping costs down. The similarity to extortion and racketeering is purely coincidental. In the end, I got my cheque the day after I notified them I was going back to work. Five months after the initial claim. The *very* next day.

So Sebastian doesn't like being tracked. Fair enough.

"Want a drink? I'll buy. I was kind of curious about —"

"Yeah, I know," he says. "Not here. Too many people."

He hands me a folded piece of paper. I start to open it, but he catches my hand.

"I said not here."

"Okaaay." I put the paper in my pocket. "Are you sure you don't — ?"

"No, I gotta go." He doesn't look at me as he scans the crowd and leaves.

I turn back to the bar, order a rye and ginger.

DELIVERY

No one but Brian has entered this living room in over three months.

Nor has the guest room housed anything but old notes, a grey, dust-gathering file cabinet, shelves of computer manuals, the forty cubic foot chest freezer he bought from his brother-in-law when they left the country. The bedroom, kitchen, storage closet, and bathroom are all more or less the same. An itemized list of contents would suffice, and he already has two of those on file, duly notarized, updated, and faxed to a personal service representative at another branch office, a person he has never met. To that person, he is nothing more than a name and a file number (Great Modern Life Insurance, Policy #52829747).

Which is as it should be. This way, if the worst were to happen — god forbid — there would be no conflict of interest. Simply an impartial adjudication. A timely and efficient settlement.

And Brian has a rock-solid policy. Tornado, flood, hurricane, any act of god or man, up to and including a lightning strike. Nothing would be lost. If someone were to invade his home right now, steal or destroy all of his belongings, even killing him in the process, his policy would remain undisturbed. His sister and brother-in-law wouldn't even have to fly back. Everything would be taken care of. As always, he has made all the smart decisions, all the right plans. Unlike his sister, just jumping up and taking off like that with no thought of the career consequences, let alone her own safety. Afghanistan, of all places. He tried to talk her out of it, but she's always been like that. Always climbing just a little higher, a little faster. At family gatherings, her litany of childhood injuries was legendary.

At 3:52 a.m. Brian rubs his eyes again, looks down at the letter, but leaves it on the coffee table. Instead, he picks up his mug, sips cold tea. He's been using the hand-addressed envelope as a makeshift coaster, and the mug has left a brown liquid ring, his middle names smudged, cursive letters from a felt-tipped pen running into indecipherable cuneiform runes. The same name he signed to the mortgage. Only ten more years, and it should be paid off in full. A sensible investment in a quiet neighbourhood, so quiet the neighbours are practically invisible. All fast asleep at this hour. If he disappeared right now, they would never know.

SALUTATION:

I check my watch — 4:07 a.m.

Look up and down the street. No one. Cross the empty gravel parking lot, read the sign with its two burnt-out letters.

Tim Horto it says, like old Timmy himself is in there but not quite completed, stepped straight off a hockey card and waiting for the nocturnal hordes to flood through that door, to ask for signatures on decades-old, fading photographs. Is he dead yet? Look back one more time: the street's still empty. Half a block away, a darkened overhead light clicks back on. Five minutes. Mental note — it lasts five minutes. I'm dawdling, I know.

Open the door, walk to the counter, order a dutchie and a decaf cappuccino with cinnamon sprinkles. The acne-scarred boy behind the counter nods, looks up at the clock then back at me.

"You're late," he says.

"I know. Sorry."

"No problem. Everyone's late the first time." He turns and calls back to the kitchen. "Sebastian! Guy's here to see you!"

"Just a minute," comes the faint response.

At the corner table, a middle-aged guy in dirty jeans and a denim jacket, curly dark-dusted-with-grey hair just reaching his collar, sips from a no-longer-steaming mug, fiddles with an unlit cigarette, and watches us. The kid behind the counter calls over.

"Oh, just light the damn thing. It's not like anyone's about to walk in."

The guy shrugs, lights his cigarette, smokes, and watches us. Sebastian comes through the door from the kitchen, wearing the same burgundy and grey uniform as the boy. He's even got one of those stupid little visors and a headset. He takes off the headset, hands it to the boy and indicates the guy in the corner with his chin.

"Don't mind Mike. He's like that sometimes." He turns to the boy. "That's everyone, then. You okay to take over for a while?"

The boy nods and puts on the headset. Sebastian gestures me around the end of the counter and leads me into the back through the kitchen, past the stainless steel convection ovens, deep fryers and mixers, past shelves of flour, raisins, oil, and other anonymous ingredients in clear plastic buckets. We don't pause, though Sebastian nods to the baker, a woman running a mixer. Lightly dusted with flour, she looks like a sculpture in progress, the shape of her hands obscured by gobbets of partially dried, cracking dough.

Through another heavy door, and we enter a long, narrow room lit by two bare bulbs, wire shelves along one wall, stacks of cardboard boxes along the other. Between the boxes and the shelves, the space is three feet wide, maybe twenty deep. Ten or twelve people sit perched on boxes, hundred-pound sacks of flour, the concrete floor. Sebastian introduces me.

"This is Jason."

Immediately to my right, the first person I recognize is Jacky. She smiles.

"Veronica. Schizophrenic. Disorganized type."

A fine line. I see. Not idiocy, lunacy. The introductions continue.

"Aidan. Bipolar. Trichotillomania."

"Mildred. Oppositional-defiant. Transvestic fetishism."

"Aloysius. Chronic depression. Obsessive compulsive with poor insight."

And so on. I recognize three more people from work, all-star developers who make more in a week than I do in a month. The rest I've never seen before, though a few seem vaguely familiar. I recognize none of the names. The introductions conclude with Sebastian.

"Schizophrenia. Paranoid type, episodic with interepisode residual symptoms."

All faces turn towards me, waiting. I clear my throat.

"Jason. Undiagnosed."

"Well, then," says Sebastian, clapping me on the shoulder. "Why don't you sit down so we can tell you a bit about what we're doing here?"

CALL TO ACTION:

Again, Brian rereads the paragraphs that follow Sebastian's
offer to Jason:

This is what Sebastian told me.
The group is called "We." We have no
desire to tear down the empire. We want to
talk, to gather and disperse information.
Present options.

Each of us has felt alone, mechanized and
constricted by--or forcibly expelled from--
the shrinking envelope of normal, the
hegemony of the real. We are not characters
on a sitcom. We are not reality tv, though
cameras have recorded our actions at every
automated teller, every convenience store,
every bank, library, and self-service gas
pump. Each of us has suspected (or discovered)
that to express our insights would be to
label ourselves as antisocial, sick, aberrant.

In an earlier age, We might have been holy
men, wise women. More recently, We might have
been denounced as witches. Now, in the age
of the statistical norm, We self-regulate.
We report our anomalous perceptions in hopes
of a cure. Diagnosis, drugs, and committal
have replaced denunciation, penance, and
execution, which in turn replaced respect,
reverence, and seclusion.

We do not postulate a conspiracy. We do
not believe there is anyone in charge.

Having formed a collective of like-minded
individuals, We harbour a growing suspicion.
We suspect there are more of us than there
are of them. We suspect that "they" do not
exist.

COMPLIMENTARY CLOSE:

Following these paragraphs, a list: social insurance number; credit card numbers and balances; birthdate, mother's maiden name; every phone call, purchase, and internet site from the last month; every one of Brian's PINS, including a few he had forgotten. The name of his first love, accompanied by a similar list. All of the information, so far as he can tell, is correct.

Below these lists, contact information, a time and a channel. And this:

```
If you choose, We can erase your files.
All of them.

Sincerely,
```

Like the address on the envelope, the signature is written in looping cursive script with a felt-tipped pen. Jason has signed it himself.

CALL BACK:

Brian checks the clock, turns on the TV, inserts a blank tape into the ancient VCR and turns it on as well. The TV flickers to life, but not the VCR. He checks the connections, toggles the switch, makes sure it's plugged in. Nothing. Sitting back down on the couch, he watches an infomercial for spray-on hair.

"I can't *believe* it! Can you *believe* this, Jane?"

"Well, Bob, it's *pretty incredible*, and at just $49.99 a can, it *sure beats* expensive transplants and other therapies."

"How long does one of those cans last, Jane?"

"Well, Bob . . ."

He sips cold tea without sugar, tastes the tannin, and waits.

At precisely 4:03 a.m., the infomercial blurs and slows, melts softly into static and white noise. The hiss of the static reminds him of running humidifiers, a hum of childhood colds, warm blankets, bedtime stories, and tuckings-in. When the static clears, he sees himself, sitting in his empty living room. He waves, and his televised self waves with him.

THE SMUT STORY (II)

For Eva S—
c/o L&P Associates
Barristers & Solicitors
Edmonton, A B

To be delivered on the occasion of her 18th birthday.[1]

10 May 2015,

Dearest Eva,
If all goes as we hope, this letter will be redundant by the time you receive it. But we have no way of guaranteeing that will be the case. So this is our insurance policy, a hedge against the unthinkable. Hopefully, its contents won't come as a complete surprise. No matter what others may have told you (especially Peter), please bear with us. You need to hear this.

[1] Editor's Note: Eva S is believed to have celebrated her 18th birthday on February 14, 2028. However, although many scholars and biographers have accepted Eva's claim that her receipt of the long-delayed "Eighteen Year Letter" — as it has come to be known — was precisely what inspired her earliest work, the question of when (and indeed whether) she actually received and read the letter, as well as her direct or indirect reactions to its contents, remain ultimately unverifiable.

For me, the memory always starts with that late spring, approaching-solstice light. The time warp kicks in the day all the clocks spring ahead, throwing everything subtly (but distinctly) off-kilter. The sun glows golden, hanging low on the horizon for hours, and the whole world becomes an instantly nostalgic, time-faded photograph of itself.

At first the effect is entirely subliminal. On a sunny afternoon, you might sit down at a cafe or patio or wherever. Doesn't matter what you're doing. Maybe you get absorbed, maybe not. Maybe you're bored as hell. But at a certain point, you look up from whatever you're doing (or not) and think, "Hey, I should eat something." Only to find the dinner hour passed, evening having long since given way to full night without the slightest hint of a transition. The light has fooled your body and mind, both retroactively awakening to the hunger that has haunted you for quite some time, only now springing full-blown into consciousness.

Every year, the slow-changing light draws me back into that same odd surrealism, a disjunction arising from a conflict between subconscious expectations and the material reality of living in this particular part of the world, at this particular time of year.

Always, it takes me like a dream.

It's May 2009 as I walk slowly, almost reluctantly, towards the reading. Mother's Day has drained these residential streets of activity, a vaguely post-apocalyptic desertion: abandoned toys on lawns, yard and gardening tools set aside, all the signs of a sudden departure. Elsewhere, restaurants are packed, parking near impossible, reservations the ultimate currency of the day. But here, Mom's night off prefigures the end of the world.

Leva materializes on the corner, a former convenience store converted to a retro Italian organic café. Broad windows across the north and west sides admit the late-afternoon light, transforming the round marble tabletops and chrome-and-plastic stools into something out of a foreign film. In the back, windowless portion of the room, a row of black-and-chrome espresso machines gleams darkly. Behind the counter, organic food, fancy coffees, and a strategically limited selection of exotic alcohols are available to those who can recognize and properly name them. Both the staff and clientele are much younger and hipper than I ever was.

As I look around, my dubious distinction as the oldest guy in the room slowly sinks in. My beige T-shirt, green hoodie, black chucks, and blue jeans suddenly feel more try-hard than inconspicuous. I had hoped to blend into the crowd, but only eight people have arrived so far. Nine including me. Recognizing no one, I take a table by myself, wishing I had brought along a book or a notebook or *something* to make me look occupied. Instead, I pretend to stare out the window, watching the half-transparent images of surrounding hipster kids reflected in the glass. Like a child hiding under covers, I'm convinced that if I don't look directly at the Monster then it won't see me, and I'll be okay. Effectively invisible.

Or perhaps I'm both monster and child. Monster in the sense of the creepy older guy, slimy old porn-junkie emerging from his basement in search of like-minded company. Child in the sense of naïveté and disorientation. Why am I even here? Sure, I've seen porn. Who hasn't? But I don't really *get* it. Perhaps my casual googling was insufficient, a proper pornographic education requiring more dedication to the form. Whatever. Everything I found was boring, too mechanistic, disconnected, misogynist, or just plain weird. Seriously. Who gets off on this stuff? But perhaps I'm missing the point. Or perhaps that *is* the point. To see if there's something *else* out there. Or rather, out here. Something between the bullshit happily-ever-after fairy tale of a romance novel (not that I've ever read one) and the empty hump and grind of internet porn. Something actually *sexy*. I don't know.

All I know is that I have never felt quite so straight as I do at this moment. Not straight as in heterosexual, but straight as in square. *Tete carré*, as the Quebecois might put it. A hapless voyeur in the land of the young. My first exposure to the very idea of sex came from playground jokes, kids who knew little more than I did, which was next to nothing. Dirty jokes whose dirtiness arose almost entirely from their incomprehensibility, the knowing chuckle we all quickly learned to fake. But these hipster-kids have grown up (insofar as they have) swimming in a virtual sea of porn. It's an everyday fact of living in a world where the internet, for as long as they can remember and beyond, *has always existed*. In such a context, even the most explicit displays of bodily extrusions and orifices, arranged in any imaginable configuration, must carry little more impact than one of those tasteless playground jokes. Or so I imagine.

I stare out the window, half-watching the slow arrivals trickle in, more hipster kids, some guy in a suit who looks almost as out of place as me. Dissociate into that all-encompassing light. Let it subsume my discomfort into the deeper surrealism of the season. Absorb.

I have no recollection of her entry.

One moment, I'm drifting awash in light, and the next she is simply there. A shadow coalescing in shades of black: T-shirt, jeans, chucks, and a hoodie. Like me, minus the awkward self-consciousness and chromatic variety. I follow her reflection in the window. Dark hair in a pageboy bob frames narrow features, her body thin to the point of boyishness yet somehow obviously, even aggressively, feminine. Can't pin down an age, so I'm assuming way too young. I risk my first direct glance of the evening to find her smiling. At me. Dark eyes and a quirked eyebrow. I revert back to my window-gazing, and by the time I look again she's taken a seat directly between me and the microphone. Alone. The crowd quiets as the reading begins.

The first reader passes in a blur. He probably thinks I'm entranced — and I am, but not by him. I can't take my eyes off Hoodie Woman. I watch her reaction to the reading, which has something to do with animal sex and the circle of life. Delèuze meets *The Lion King* meets Nietzsche or some such nonsense. She looks . . . nonplussed, and I can practically hear her thoughts. *Porn and erotica? This?*

I agree. Deleuze? I mean, I get the sapiophile thing, but that's still one hell of a stretch. He could have at least gone with Irigaray or Cixous. Thankfully, the reader finishes quickly and scurries back to his seat, his departure accompanied by polite applause.

Next up, an older woman reads a piece about porn-watching teenaged boys, a note-perfect depiction of their reactions to hardcore porn in the semi-public social setting of a basement rec-room. Her wry description of the wah-wah guitars, bad dialogue, and orifice-filling frenzy of bad porn makes me chuckle, and her recounting of the boys' crass overcompensation for their own sexual inexperience — manifesting in a series of increasingly tasteless and even downright offensive 14-year-old-boy commentary — makes me cringe in recognition. Yet even through the most explicit scenes, she keeps her eyes fixed on the text before her, no shift in expression beyond the occasional introspective smile. As if she's simply watching these events unfold on a small eight-and-a-half-by-eleven screen and reporting them back to us in real time. Beneath the satire, I hear an undercurrent of sympathy for the boys' naïveté, and I wonder if she has teenaged boys of her own. If so, I doubt they realize how lucky they are.

Hoodie Woman tilts her head back and closes her eyes, exposing the delicate curve of her throat. Lips part, breath visibly deepening as her hands open wide. Fingers grasping at air as the piece winds to its end, a final image of the boys' inevitably impending wet dreams. On the final line, her hands clench and eyes snap open, locking onto the reader. A silent, full-body shiver, then another, and her fists release. The reader looks up for the first time and freezes, snared by Hoodie Woman's eyes, that focused stare. The reader's eyes widen, and I have to look away.

When I look back, the reader has turned bright red, her gaze pinned to the floor before her. She murmurs a closing thank you, and the applause is immediate and enthusiastic as she walks swiftly back to her seat, still avoiding all eye contact. The emcee encourages us to refresh our drinks for the next set and immediately follows her own advice, beelining to the counter for a glass of white wine. She downs it, orders another, then sips the second while casting occasional, darting glances over at Hoodie Woman. So it's not just me.

As the slow wave of between-sets conversation rises, anticipation crackles through the room like an approaching prairie storm. Everyone talks at once, trying (and failing) to defuse that unspoken, building tension. Hoodie Woman sits alone at the eye of the storm, surveying the room and its inhabitants, sipping her red wine in silence. I also sit in silence, racking my brain for some way to start a conversation. I have to meet her. As I half-rise to walk over and give it a shot, a voice emerges from the surrounding hum.

"Is this seat taken?" A thin blonde woman stands next to me, her hand on the back of the unoccupied chair where I've set my jacket. She looks nervous. "I mean, if you're saving it . . ."

"No. No, not at all." I smile (reassuringly, I hope), transfer my jacket from the empty chair to the back of my own, and again begin to stand. "In fact, if you could save my seat . . ." But now Hoodie Woman is deep in conversation with one of the organizers. Too slow.

I sit back down.

"Thanks!" says the blonde. "I mean, if you're sure that's okay."

"No really, I'd love the company." Still, she hesitates. "I was actually feeling a bit conspicuous. You know, guy sitting alone at a porn reading." Sure, that'll make her feel real comfortable. "I uh . . . I mean, really, it's no problem. All yours." I push the chair in her direction.

She sits but seems paralyzed by the question of where to put her jacket and purse. The stutter-step rhythm of her movements reminds me of a squirrel. She tries the table first, then pauses. A quick half-move towards her lap, another longer pause, and a decisive flurry of action, purse under chair, coat draped over the back. "I mean, I got here late," she resumes, settled now but speech still echoing that same stuttering rhythm. "And I stood at the bar for the first set, but." A half-second pause, then all in one breath, "But then I noticed this seat but I wasn't sure if it was free or not so I just waited for the break and now . . . Well . . . Hi."

We shake hands. More organizers surround Hoodie Woman. And though they outnumber her four to one, they're the ones who look nervous.

"So have you been to a lot of these things?" The blonde's question pulls me back. "I mean, is this how they usually go?" She's cute, I realize, but not intimidatingly so. A hint of hot-librarian with muted vegan undertones. Her glasses are big, round, clunky things, and she wears no makeup. Like her clothes, the glasses are too plain and lacking in irony to be fashionable with this crowd. Not vintage, just aging and a bit out of date. Like me.

"Actually, I have no idea," I admit. "It's my first time too. It's . . . interesting."

"That's one word for it." She smiles, calmer now, and catches me glancing at Hoodie Woman, who is laughing with the last reader, the woman who couldn't meet her eye just a few minutes ago. The blonde chin-nods. "Friend of yours?"

I blush. "No, we've never . . . I mean, I guess I just . . ."

"Oh, I know exactly what you mean." She chuckles, openly staring at the object of my not-as-covert-as-I-thought attention. "You know, for the life of me I couldn't tell you what the first two readers looked like?"

The emcee's introduction of the next set cuts off my response.

A woman in the audience hands off the newborn in her lap to the man beside her, stands, and approaches the microphone. She has that T-shirt-and-overalls look of a new mom, totally at ease in her own physicality, and she launches directly into a piece exploring pre-, during-, and post-pregnancy sex in explicit and erotic detail. The blonde blushes right up to her hairline, and for the first time tonight I feel like the voyeur I earlier imagined myself to be. This reader makes unflinching eye-contact with individual audience members, some for just a few words, others for a full line or more. She saves Hoodie Woman for last, finally meeting her gaze and holding it through an entire stanza, mingling images of breastfeeding, labour, and orgasm to close on a sustained climax of milk and blood and cum.

No one makes a sound.

A single clap. Then another. Hoodie Woman applauds alone, still holding that gaze. Then she smiles and nods, a brief head-dip of respect freeing the reader to deliver two ringing thank yous, one to Hoodie Woman, the second to the room at large. The answering applause is thunderous, including a few hoots and whistles. The reader returns to her seat, retrieves her child, and nods back to Hoodie Woman over the nestling newborn's head. Then she calmly unhooks an overall strap, lifts her shirt, and latches the child to her breast to nurse.

Still applauding, the emcee returns to the microphone and introduces the final reader as "Mr. T. Boop." I think I am ready for anything. Until Hoodie Woman pushes back her chair, stands, and slowly walks to the front. She takes her time, lightly touching the emcee's arm and leaning forward to whisper something in her ear before turning to face us.

No, not us. Me. Her eyes lock on mine. A wave of vertigo.

Then the adrenaline jolt. Accelerated heart rate, breath turning shallow and fast, a deep *hop* in the gut as that swooping moment of freefall stretches. A powerful desire to hide, and a strong thread of fear. Fear and panic and paralysis (still pinned by those eyes), and at first the only thought I can muster is *oh fuck*. Then: *Holy shit, I really want this person.*

And it scares the shit out of me.

Her eyes expand, pupils dilating impossibly large as the room fades and recedes. Darkness creeps in at the edge of my vision, the chair beneath me and the table I lean on turning abstract, fluid, and nebulous. And though I know I must still be sitting in the chair, still gripping the table, my feet and hands float in empty space as gravity contorts, convulses, and vanishes. Her face a final beacon in the surrounding darkness. Then that disappears too.

I shake my head. Blink furiously. No change. Just the strangely muted sound of my own breathing. It doesn't echo or reverberate. It is *absorbed*. As if the darkness were a sponge, soaking up every light, sound, touch, and smell to leave me floating alone in perfect isolation. Except for her. I can't see her, but I know she's here.

The darkness is warm and humid. If it weren't for the slightest warm breath against my corneas, I wouldn't know if my eyes were open or closed.

Close them for several seconds. Deliberately turn my head. Open.

The room shimmers like heat-wave haze over summer blacktop then slowly swims into focus. The espresso machines in the back, the Euro-minimalist décor, the setting sun a bit lower, but still there. The light, the world, and all the objects within it have returned. But the silence remains. No background chatter. No clinking of dishes, cutlery, or glasses, no whispered orders at the front counter. No soft rustle of people shifting in their seats.

I scan the audience to either side, carefully avoiding even the slightest glance towards the front of the room. Some stare blankly in the same direction I avoid. Are they trapped in the space I just escaped? Others, like me, blink and shake their heads, averting their eyes as I do. The latter shy away from direct eye contact, as if that singular gaze might be contagious, each pair of eyes a trap waiting to be sprung. A flurry of noise and motion at the far end of the room as first one man, then a woman, then others, slam down their glasses and mugs, hastily gather their belongings, and head for the door. A few more hurried exits, the door slamming once, twice, three times. The full exodus takes no more than a minute or two. A final slam of the door, and silence returns. The only sound, that of the crowd's soft, slow respiration. Only a few remain who have thus far avoided (or escaped) the gravity well of Tia's eyes. Any who glance in her direction, however briefly, are instantly caught.

Finally, she speaks. A whisper so soft it should be hard to hear. But it's not.

"This story is not for reading, but for telling. Not for you, but for your lover. This is the story of a story of a story ..."

I listen to Tia's story, which is also my story. It is beyond porn. No distanced, controlling camera. No distance at all. Not apart from me, but a part of me. A reflective, amplifying feedback loop. Her voice lifts me up and pulls me in, a wave of sound evading all internal censors to draw out my most intimate sensual fantasies, my most secret desires. Drawing them out only to return them to me, shared and multiplied in the amplifying echo of a lover's growing arousal. In response to this story. My story. A story of lips and skin and tongue. Of taste and touch. Slowly, with a growing (yet achingly restrained) urgency, the story builds.

A ragged gasp at my side pulls me back.

The blonde surfaces as I did, shaking her head and breathing heavily. Her shoulders hunch, white-knuckled hands gripping the marble tabletop. A pause, then she pushes herself up to look around the room. Our eyes meet, and we mirror each other's confusion across the small table as Tia's story continues. Progressively colonizing our senses, it expands. I can still see the blonde breathing — almost hyperventilating now — but the sound is gone. She looks down at her feet, squares her shoulders, and takes a long, slow breath. When she looks back up, she smiles and shrugs as if to say, *Hey, if you can't beat 'em . . .* Then she takes one more deep breath like a swimmer about to dive, and turns to face Tia.

And though my resistance is waning, breath grown ragged and muscles tensing under the story's growing influence, I can still focus just enough to see the full process. The electric jolt of initial contact, her entire body stiffening. A soft gasp (seen not heard), eyes widening, pupils instantly dilated. Then the tension passes, shoulders release, and her lips part slightly, curving upwards as she willingly surrenders to her own world-engulfing arousal.

In that moment, she is absolutely fucking gorgeous.

Time and space vanish. Only the story remains.

The room slowly coalesces in half-silvered café windows, and as Tia concludes with thanks and an exhortation for us to share our own stories, I watch its reflection, returning. I have forgotten nothing, details as fresh and vivid now as they will remain for years to come. But the compulsion to watch Tia has vanished. Now, I want to see everyone else.

A few formerly occupied tables sit entirely empty. Those who remain stare as openly as I do. And suddenly everyone — every single person — is inexpressibly beautiful. I meet several pairs of eyes and never once feel the urge to look away. Around the room, glances meet, and these universally flushed cheeks clearly have nothing to do with embarrassment. My eyes wander back across the room to settle on the blonde beside me. Like every other person, she sits entirely unchanged. Like every other person, she is transformed. Our eyes meet and hold. Then she smiles, and I smile back. And we begin to talk.

First, we talk about the story. She shares her version, I mine. They start off the same but rapidly diverge into completely different (though equally explicit) narratives. And when first a man, then two more women and another man join us, the sharing expands to incorporate each new arrival's story, divergences multiplying and growing ever wilder. Given the content, the conversation is strangely effortless. At first we avoid touching, but incidental contacts accumulate, prompting shared smiles, more expansive gestures. Hands brushing across the table, a chance jostling of shoulders, a hand on a shoulder or the back of a neck.

When the subject of Tia herself comes up — and here there is some debate as to whether it was *Tia* or *Tio* — we discover that she, like her story, manifested differently for each person. Depending on the viewer, she was male, female, trans, androgynous, fat, thin, both light and dark haired, light and dark skinned. One woman insists she was wearing a mask. No one seems particularly concerned by these discrepancies. We're more interested in the stories.

Only much later does it occur to one of the women to wonder if Tio (or Tia) might want to join our conversation. But when we finally look around and try to locate her (or him), we find that he (or she) is gone.

• • •

Not much more to tell, really. Where the audience had arrived in quiet singles, pairs, and trios, it left in talkative quads, quints, and sextuples. Our group adjourned to Jamie's place — yes, *that* Jamie[2] — where we continued sharing stories. No longer merely recounting, we started embellishing with increasingly collaborative interjections. I think it was Peter who started that, though some of the others remember it differently. By that time, everyone was talking at once so it's hard to say for sure. Some additions were funny, others downright strange. Later, none of us could pinpoint exactly when we shifted from telling to showing.

When the six of us awoke the next morning, there was no sense of awkwardness as we dressed, exchanged phone numbers, and agreed to keep in touch. And incredibly, we did. Except for Peter. Within a week he stopped returning our calls, and the number he gave us was disconnected a few weeks later. That was disappointing, but aside from your mother no one was particularly worried. Right from the start, Peter seemed more solid than anyone, generally grounded, stable, and competent in the world. Shows how much we knew.

Later, as your mother's pregnancy became more apparent — and yes, of course she was "the blonde" — it seemed

---

2 Editor's Note: Although Jamie's identity has never been confirmed, it seems reasonable to assume that this is the same person Eva S often refers to in her own writings as "Uncle" — or occasionally "Auntie" — Jamie, who is generally assumed to be one of her five co-parents. If one believes Eva S's version of her own history.

only natural for her and Jamie to rent a house, and the rest of us moved in one at a time as our respective leases ran out. And then there was you. How to explain these last five years? The incredible moment of your arrival, the brief but intense battle we fought to have all five of us present in the delivery room when the home-birth turned complicated and we ended up in a hospital after all? Those first few months? You have changed us all, and (almost) all for the better. We foresaw none of this, but we wouldn't change a thing. Well, except for Peter. As you no doubt know by now, he didn't take it well.

The rest, I'm sure, is fairly obvious. Or should be if things have gone as we hope. But Peter's raising a stink again. At first it was just letters to the editor, a few op-eds, all that crap about the reading. We tried to contact him, left messages inviting him to come visit any time, that we considered him as much your parent as any of us. But he got it in his head that people "like us" (whatever that means) aren't fit to raise a child. After he got married, he upped his game, turned the whole thing into a legal battle, starting with (failed) demands for paternity testing (which would have required your mother's consent), then suing for custody on broader "moral" grounds. For a while none of it went anywhere, but now he's got some serious backing. Some conservative "family values" group, which we're thinking must mean he hasn't told them everything. And that's good, might give us some leverage if push comes to shove. Still, even if they ditch Peter along the way, these family value thugs might still go after us in court, try to set a legal precedent or something. Thus this insurance policy.

We *hope* that none of this is necessary, that we're being overly paranoid and worrying for nothing. But the fact is, if you're receiving this letter, we have no way of knowing what you may think of us by now. A lot can happen in thirteen years. And we wanted to make sure you at least knew your own history. You deserve at least that much. So if we haven't been able to tell you this story ourselves, we hope you will at least consider the possibility that there is *absolutely nothing wrong or shameful about you and where you came from.* Whatever second thoughts Peter may have had, and whatever he may have told you, you were conceived and raised — insofar and for as long as we were able — in a space of joy and love and celebration.

We also figured this was probably the closest you could get to meeting Tia (or Tio). And since she (or he) is in some ways as much your parent as any one of the six of us — and yes, that includes Peter — we thought you at least deserved to know. First, where you came from, and how, and under what circumstances. Second, that we believe in you. Even now, I can hear you laughing in the next room. And for this I will always be grateful. May you always hold onto that incredible joy. And may you never have to receive this letter.

BOUNDARY PROBLEMS

"What about Patches?"

Michael half-heartedly eavesdrops on the conversation in the common room as he sorts his gear into the battered trunk at the foot of the bed. Half-heartedly, because although he's just met these people today, he's heard it a thousand times. At nineteen, with three seasons under his belt, he feels like a weathered veteran. It's a new camp, but everything is familiar. The usual cruddy old mattress on the usual squeaky old cot, Salvation Army–grade furniture in the common room of the staff cabin, the ubiquitous sand and grit that will reappear within moments of sweeping the grey-tiled floor. And of course, the inevitable hormone-driven partner scramble.

"Patches is a skank."

That would be Caesar, Michael's new roommate. Big guy, not too bright. Ideal, really. Unlikely to want to stay up late discussing inane, sophomoric philosophies or anything like that. A real straightforward guy. Probably plays football. Linebacker maybe. Caesar continues holding forth in his uninspired, predictable way.

"That pouty thing? Classic case of cocksucker's cramp."

Yes, almost certainly a football player. Obviously not used to rejection. Michael recalls the bus ride up, Patches giving Caesar the brush-off. He also remembers noticing Erin, Patches' tall, quiet friend in the next seat over watching him watching them, how his own eye-rolling mockery of the transparent drama prompted a brief grin before she looked down and away, dark curls falling forward too late to hide her reaction. When Erin looked up again, she stared blankly out the window, watching the endless green blur of Northern Ontario treescape with an intensity bordering on neurotic. Kind of cute, but then again, Saybo had smiled too. And she hadn't looked away. As more voices join the common room conversation, Michael abandons his eavesdropping, anticipating and half-planning his next move in the game of musical beds otherwise known as orientation week.

The next day Jan, the blond and wind-burned ex-hippie camp director formally re-introduces himself (Jan like "yawn," not Jan like "January") and organizes a team-building workshop in what he calls the *Assafay Duben* massage technique. An obvious pun for the bilinguals in the crowd. Michael tries to catch Saybo's eye in the partner-scramble but ends up paired with Blink. Blink is short, round, and cheerful, and listens attentively as Jan explains the point of the exercise, which he says is to practice the art of explicitly *non*-sexual touch. Michael tunes out the recycled wisdoms of *The Celestine Prophecy* and other dubious sources as the director suggests (predictably) that yes, everyone needs touch and affection, but these things don't always have to be sexual.

Blink's pale flesh yields like dough, and Michael's fingers sink in well past the first knuckle before encountering even the slightest resistance. Like an embarrassingly liberal father, Jan produces a pair of magnets to illustrate the virtue of taking things slow. He holds the magnets with matching poles facing to demonstrate the correspondent repulsion, suggesting that this sort of deferred, inverted tension should be allowed to build over time. To Michael, this sounds more like foreplay advice than a way to avoid the summer-long bed-hopping extravaganza, itself the unsurprising result of taking a collection of hormone-pumped eighteen-to-twentysomethings out in the woods and giving them inordinate amounts of responsibility.

Halfway through his explanation, Jan fumbles the magnets, which instantly flip around and clap together. Patches seizes the moment to cry out once full-voiced, arching her back, then holds that eyes-closed, skyward-facing pose for just a little too long before slumping bonelessly to the floor, strategically ass-ripped jeans conspicuously foregrounded by her carefully calculated sprawl. Erin — trapped at the centre of attention by her partner's faux-orgasmic outburst — turns bright red, but Jan just smiles and says something about the necessary release of tension. Everyone laughs, even Michael.

On the third night of orientation, a Harley rumbles in the gravel lane just as dinner finishes, and Michael watches Jan bound down the dining hall steps to greet the leather-clad biker with a flying hug. The biker easily catches the smaller man in mid-air, laughing and shaking his shaven head as he extricates himself from Jan's enthusiastic embrace.

At nine o'clock sharp the next morning, the biker is revealed as the Therapeutic Crisis Intervention instructor, here to teach them the practical and legal frameworks for dealing with *youth at risk*. As Michael learned during his day-long group interview a month before, this camp deals exclusively with what he thinks of as *System Kids*. He's worked with kids like this before, but always just one or two at a time, and he has never before received any specialized training. By contrast, all of the kids at this camp have been removed from their families, some having been abused, others arrested, many both. This removal itself is what puts them *at risk*. Statistically speaking, the *risk* covers a host of unpleasant long-term outcomes, from drug use to prostitution to plain old mind-numbing poverty. And this is new. It's part of why Michael took the job, to combat his own growing cynicism, try to do something real for once.

The biker is a self-confessed adrenaline junkie with black belts in several martial arts, and he always refers to the kids as *clients*. On the first day, he teaches the staff how to recognize conflict and keep it from escalating, or better yet, how to keep it from developing in the first place. He also teaches them techniques for managing conflicts that have already escalated: active listening, basic mediation, the use of I-statements. All the usual stuff. Whenever his audience seems to be losing focus, the biker spices his lengthy theoretical explanations with anecdotes, like that of the eight-year-old girl who stapled a pencil-crayon drawing through her teacher's shirt and into his stomach. For a family portrait assignment, she had sketched a disturbingly detailed penis and testicles, all deep blues and purples. When the teacher suggested she might want to reconsider her choice of subject matter, she went ballistic. First with the stapler, then stabbing with pencil crayons. Luckily, says the biker, the blood loss was minor, since the holes were relatively small, and the pencil crayons didn't hit anything vital.

Later, a small audience of counsellors lingers over coffee, captivated by stories of the biker's checkered past. He describes his current day job as an ambulance driver in clinical, startling detail: the sickening crack of a woman's ribs and sternum breaking the first time he administered CPR on a live human being, the strange sensation of open palms sinking through broken bones and deep into the suddenly-yielding chest cavity

beneath. These stories naturally branch out into further anecdotes balanced on that same thin line between life and death,
control and chaos. He's had near-misses on the bike, been
attacked by all manner of violent clients, dragged countless
not-quite-corpses from spectacularly mangled vehicles. He
has watched people die. Like a sunrise over mountains, these
stories cast a sudden glaring light, exposing the sharply limited horizons of Michael's own first-hand experience.

The next day, dining hall tables are pushed aside to leave
space for exercises, and the counsellors learn the precisely
regulated methods of physical restraint for out-of-control
clients — basket holds for the smaller kids, two-person take-
downs for the bigger ones. These restraints, says the biker,
are always a sign of failure. Any person who uses one has
already screwed up every technique he's taught them so far.
But restraints will be necessary, because sooner or later everyone screws up. In these situations, restraints are intended
to prevent three types of harm: to bystanders, to the client,
or to you.

"So," says the instructor, folding heavily muscled arms over
comic-book-worthy pectorals, "what do you do if a client comes
at you with a knife?" The situations they discuss now are
hypothetical but not unlikely. Two weeks from now, Michael
will see a cherubically cute six-year-old stab his counsellor
with a fork at breakfast, tines sinking deep into the fleshy pad
at the base of the thumb. These things happen.

The counsellors role-play two-person restraints in groups
of three, taking turns playing staff and client, taking down or
being taken down. Both staff and client roles are invigorating:
the perfect flow of getting it right and effortlessly pinning a
"client," the gravity-defying rush of being swept from one's
feet and deposited solidly yet painlessly on the hardwood
floor. In the latter case, Michael unconsciously cooperates with
Patches and Erin's takedown, amazed at the gentleness of his

landing and turned on enough to be relieved the restraint ends facedown. But the instructor notices Michael's complicity and makes them do it again. This time, when the girls pin him in spite of his genuine resistance, the result is so sudden and unexpected that even his libido has no time to react. And when he tries to escape as per the biker's instructions, Michael finds he cannot.

Later, taking a break from the physical drilling, the biker has a new question. "What if a client offers to tell you a secret, but only if you promise to keep it?"

A three-sided debate ensues. One faction argues they would never break a promise once given, another that they would give the promise then break it, yet another that they would refuse to make the promise in the first place. As it turns out, what to say is entirely up to the individual. The important part is to understand that even if you do make that promise, it isn't worth a damn. If a child discloses abuse, you are legally required to report it. No exceptions. It's not up to counsellors to decide the truth or falsehood of such claims, and although belief isn't required, overt skepticism is not an option. Every claim must be treated as true.

⁂

Two days before the kids arrive, everyone hunkers down in the women's staff cabin for an all-night movie marathon. A dozen counsellors sprawl around the room, pillows, cushions, and sleeping bags spread about in the summer camp equivalent of a Turkish harem. Caesar and Saybo whisper conspiratorially on a couch in the back while Patches flirts with Tex and Ellie on another couch along the side of the room. On the floor just back from the TV, Blink sits next to Erin, who massages Michael's neck and shoulders. Other staff sit or lie scattered around the room in similar pairs, trios, and quadruples.

Partway through *Apocalypse Now*, Michael notices that Caesar and Saybo have disappeared — off making out again, no doubt. Not even a day since they first hooked up, and already Michael has walked in on them twice. The rising cadences of *Ride of the Valkyries* fill the air and munitions explode onscreen as Michael relaxes into Erin's massage. Her fingers deftly seek out each individual knot of tension, pressuring them first into submission and then release. Erin is six feet tall, with strong hands, and has already earned the nickname *Zeus*, short for *masseuse*. It isn't unusual for people to fall asleep during Erin's massages, so Michael lets his eyes fall shut as she draws his head back to rest on her stomach and switches from neck and shoulders to scalp and temples. Drifting, Michael recalls his own abortive hookup with Saybo two days ago, the belated discovery of her absolutely abysmal taste in music and astonishingly bad make-out technique. Apparently, not all girls are good kissers. Even so, he has to cross his legs to mask the memory-induced erection, which has the unfortunate side effect of revealing his continued wakefulness. But Erin ignores his movement, abandons the massage entirely, and gently crosses her arms over his chest. Where it rests between Erin's legs, Michael's back feels suggestively warm, and he fervently hopes that tonight Caesar and Saybo have found a new make-out spot.

First session, Michael is assigned to the *zoomers* — so-called because eleven- and twelve-year-old boys tend to *zoom* everywhere they go. They never stop moving. Michael's companion in this trial by exhaustion will be Tex, who (incredibly) has almost as much energy as the kids, while the matching female cabin is co-counselled by Blink and Patches. An interesting combination, but Blink and Michael are quickly becoming friends, and Patches turns out to be surprisingly pragmatic when the kids are around. When the boys arrive, they tumble off the bus in a collective fart-joking, hyperactive ball of prepubescent energy. Michael and Tex quickly discover the ambivalent joys of a constant caffeine intake, along with the unexpected utility of having an extremely hot female counsellor as a last resort backup. The boys may be prepubescent, but even they aren't entirely immune to Patches' charms.

The daily routine quickly devolves into a constant stream of physical activities and games, from swimming races, splash-fights, and canoe wars to freeze tag, archery competitions, and kamikaze earth-ball soccer. The all-time favourite of these is the game-game, a meta-game in which oversized cardboard-box "dice" are rolled to pick the elements from which a new game will be invented. For sanity breaks, there's the occasional game of graveyard, with all the kids playing dead, the last one to move or betray any sign of life winning. (This invariably ends with the accumulated losers tickling the last few finalists until someone snaps.) Or the ever-popular "nature walks," consisting primarily of searches for wriggly, squirmy things with which to torment the girls. Plus campfires, overnights, silly songs, marshmallow roasts, cookouts, and ghost stories. And fart jokes. Lots of fart jokes.

Although he laughs at the fart jokes and participates in activities with good-natured enthusiasm, Jonas stands out. A skinny little guy with a shock of white-blond, sun-bleached hair, and a broad habitual grin flashing bright against his nut-brown tan, he immediately bounces up to rejoin the game with a smile even when the kamikaze earth-ball flings him several feet through the air to land hard on the playing field grass. But outside of group games and required physical activities, Jonas maintains a contemplative silence that eludes his more rambunctious cabin-mates. During rest hour, he quietly stakes his claim as the camp's unofficial chess champion. Every day, Caesar and Jonas face each other across a small magnetic board on the plastic mattress of a lower bunk. And every day, the eighteen-year-old sailing director loses to the eleven-year-old boy. Jonas never gloats or trash-talks, merely smiles, shakes hands, and packs up the game for the next day's match. Caesar tries to make a joke out of it, laughing and playing the good sport, but Michael can see how badly he wants to beat that kid.

When Jonas's father shows up on Visitor Sunday, Michael forgets the man's name the moment he's introduced and mentally dubs him *Dad* for convenience. Jonas and Dad look alike, especially if Michael imagines away the father's forked and braided beard. Both are achingly thin, the same small, wiry muscles clearly visible under deep-tanned skin. Jonas is just a skinny kid, but on Dad the build has more of a heroin-chic effect. Michael doesn't see any tracks though, and since Dad goes shirtless in cut-offs and sandals it's hard to imagine where he might hide them. Jonas is even quieter than usual when Dad's around. But he does as he's told and spends the day with his father, reducing Michael's cabin by one until he reappears in the dining hall for dinner, rejoining the group to eat in an envelope of silence. Then again, lots of kids do that on Visitor Sundays, the introspective aura of the day casting a strange pall over the normally boisterous evening meal.

At lights-out, the cabin loudmouth makes a joke at Jonas's expense. Standard momma-joke: *Your momma's so fat* . . . The line vanishes from memory even as it's spoken. Jonas snarls and pounces without warning, flattens the loudmouth with a roundhouse to the ear, then jumps on him, landing several more flailing body blows before Michael pulls him off. The momma-joker, twice Jonas's size and still on his ass, scrabbles away across the floor, his face distorted by a cartoonish shock that would be funny if Michael wasn't so busy wrestling Jonas into a basket hold and carrying him out the door. Jonas keeps kicking and shouting the whole way down to the waterfront.

The kid's stronger than he looks, and though it's easy enough to lift him off his feet and into the air, Michael can barely keep a grip on those squirming wrists as Jonas flings his weight violently from side to side. At the waterfront, Michael completes the last step of the basket hold, setting the boy in front of him on the sand, then sitting behind him with legs on either side to loop his own ankles over the boy's kicking feet. It's not as graceful as the practice sessions, but it works. And at this distance, Jonas's shouting is less likely to disturb the other junior boy cabins, which stand bunched at the top of the hill like a convoy of Conestoga wagons circled round for the night.

Michael and Jonas face the lake, looking down over the five stepped terraces of sand held in place by banks of railway ties, the swimming dock at the bottom. Michael had hoped the sound of lapping waves might help calm the boy, but there's no chance of hearing them over Jonas's child-pitched shouts and growls, which show no signs of abating. Michael can barely make out the words.

"LetmeGOletmeGOLETmeGO! RrrAH! LETMEGO!"

"I can't let go until you calm down." Michael speaks in measured tones, close enough to Jonas's ear that there's no need to raise his voice. "Do you think you're ready to calm down?" Jonas snarls and slams his head back, and Michael twists his head aside just in time to avoid a fat lip, barely maintaining his grip on the squirming boy. He tries again. "Is there anything I can do? Anything that might help?"

Another snarl. With a sudden surge, Jonas kicks one leg free, and Michael grunts with the effort required to re-hook the boy's ankle and bring him back under control. When the leg is pinned once more, Jonas falls still, and Michael can feel the boy's pulse racing against his chest as they both gasp for breath.

"Okay . . . Okay, fair enough. You just let me know when you're ready."

The moon sketches a rippling path across the water. The sand, freshly churned by Jonas's struggle, is cold and damp, and Michael can feel the boy starting to shiver. Poor kid isn't even wearing a shirt, just his pyjama bottoms. He must be freezing. After a lengthy silence broken only by the sound of waves lapping railway ties thirty feet away, Jonas speaks.

"Okay," he says. "I'm ready."

"You sure?"

"Yeah."

Michael lets him go, and they walk back to the cabin in silence. The rest of the kids are already asleep. The incident is never repeated, and though Michael has a talk with the momma-joker the next morning, he never presses Jonas for an explanation. It's not a lack of curiosity, or even a matter of respect. Michael continually imagines scenarios, explanations for what might have set Jonas off like that. If he wanted to, he could probably get a look at the case files, or at least ask Jan. But at the same time, Michael feels he's developed a tenuous bond with this boy, a fragile connection predicated on the maintenance of this open, receptive silence.

Cabin-duty is only every second night, so Michael and Erin coordinate their nights off, talking and making out until dawn pinks the sky as they return to wake their respective cabins for the long day ahead. Always in private and in his mind, Michael uses Erin's real name. They smoke cigars and corn-cob pipes purchased from the dollar store in town, emphasizing conversational points with puffs of smoke and jabs of glowing embers. Generally, they agree that the world is pretty much stupid, though they often argue as to precisely how and why. Michael memorizes her face and body from every angle, the light dusting of freckles across the bridge of her nose, the secret angle where the curve of her neck meets that strong jawline. And he compulsively imagines those parts of her body he has never seen. He isn't impatient, exactly, but they haven't gone that far yet, and he looks forward to the revelation.

During the day, both are irritable and punchy with lack of sleep, stumbling through the constant rounding cycle of camp life. Archery, arts and crafts, swimming, canoeing, and all the rest blur into one long, endless task, merely marking time until they can shed their daytime personae in favour of their true selves, this private nocturnal life. Jan pulls them each aside for half-hearted individual scoldings, reminding them in that Hippie Dad admonishing-yet-supportive way of his that they need to get some sleep or they'll be no good to anyone, least of all themselves. And Jan is so nice about it, so thoroughly reasonable that in the moment of that conversation they can't help but agree. Yet when the next night off arrives, the director's advice burns off like morning mist and the cycle resumes. They are like Jan's magnets, their mutual attraction the product of a physical law that cannot be denied.

The first session ends, and for thirty-six glorious hours of changeover, the campers are gone. Addicts on a binge, they spend every moment together. In the next session, Michael and Blink will be running the Leaders in Training program, a much-coveted position in which they will take ten fifteen-year-olds on a ten-day canoe trip through Algonquin Park. Michael realizes that this is Jan's way of separating him from Erin, but this knowledge has no effect beyond making their remaining nights off all the more intense, as together they count down the hours to Michael's departure. The day before he leaves, Erin swaps nights off with her co-counsellor, smoking and watching as he patches the last of the canoes with fast-drying epoxy. And at some point during the night,

Michael realizes that although this isn't his first relationship — or even his first summer romance for that matter — he
has begun thinking of Erin as his first Real Girlfriend. As if
all memories of preceding girls have turned to smoke and
ashes, like so many spent cigarettes tossed into a blazing
campfire.

When Chris shows up alone at the portage, unsteadily soloing
his canoe against stiff headwinds, Michael's first reaction is
bewilderment. Chris is high-functioning autistic, and Michael
has been pairing him with Brow to even out the canoeing partners. Michael holds the gunnels as Chris reaches the shore and
climbs out, then unloads the gear and hauls the canoe up on
the sand as Chris explains in his characteristic monotone that
Brow decided to stay behind at the lunch site.

"What do you mean 'stay behind,' Chris? What *exactly* did
he say?"

"He said gimme that pack you go on I'm staying here you
go," says Chris. "And then he said go on and paddle your own
damn self for once go on now go you heard me go."

"Fuck!" shouts Michael. "Blink! I need to go get Brow. You
okay to load everyone up and take them through on your
own?" Chris jumps at the shout, then wanders off towards
the rest of the campers, who sit lounging by the packs and
canoes at the trailhead.

"Sure, no problem. Where's Brow? Is everything okay?"

"Not here, that's where!" Michael calls over his shoulder
as he ditches his gear and pushes Chris's canoe back into the
water. "Sounds like he's having some kind of snit. Chris can
explain. You go on ahead and we'll catch up." Then he shoves
off and heads out across the choppy northern Ontario lake to
fetch the ornery little prick.

Not that he's all that little. Barely fifteen, and already Brow matches Michael's own 180 pounds. Problem is, the kid's also stubborn as hell. As Michael wrestles the canoe around and settles in for some hard paddling, he wonders what set Brow off this time. No telling, but it's always something. Hell of a chip on that shoulder. Never should have gone along with the nickname thing. It seemed harmless enough when he started insisting everyone call him by that stupid name, ostensibly in homage to the thick mono-brow over the bridge of his nose but really in imitation of the staff nicknames. Kind of endearing in a hapless fifteen-year-old kind of way. Until he started bossing the other kids around, acting like the nickname alone granted him de facto staff authority. Little fucker's temper doesn't help either, keeps half the campers and even some staff pussyfooting around for fear of setting him off. Last time he flipped out, it took three big guys just to hold him down. He'd better not try to pull that shit now, or he'll see just how far it will get him. Holding up the whole goddamn group. Fuck. Just have to get him and bring him back. That's all. And stay calm. Remember, no matter how big — or incredibly *frustrating* — he may be, he's still just a kid.

Michael pours on the speed, cursing when his paddle catches a wave side-on and splashes water into the boat. Still, the tailwind's helping, and the burn of exertion in his arms and shoulders feels good, matches his racing pulse as he approaches the lunch site twenty minutes later and spots Brow perched on a boulder well back from the water. In his rush to land, Michael hops too quickly from the canoe, capsizes it less than a foot from shore, and slips and falls to his knees on the slick shale below. The shock of cold water makes his breath catch, waves splashing up to his chest before he regains his footing, wades unsteadily ashore, and hauls the swamped canoe up onto the rocks behind him. He flips it over, dumping out the last of the water, then stomps soggily up the slope towards his wayward charge. Brow's sleeping roll, still tightly tied and wrapped in waterproofing plastic, leans against the boulder.

At the top of the rise, Michael pauses and resolves not to shout.

"Benjamin," he says, using Brow's real name. Calmly. "Chris said you decided to stay behind." A little louder, but that's okay. Still not shouting. "So you want to tell me what the *hell* you think you're doing?"

Brow hunches his shoulders, scowls, and glares down at Michael from his seat atop the rock. Then launches in. "Why do I always get stuck paddling with Chris? It's not fair. He's a shitty paddler, and he's lazy. All he does is talk to himself, and every two minutes I have to tell him to start paddling again. And even when he does paddle, he's a lily-dipper. He's lazy and stupid and weird, and I'm not paddling with him any more." By the time he's finished, his scowl has shifted to more of a pout. Poor Brow. So hard done by.

"So what, now you're just going to sit here on a rock and sulk?"

"I've got a plan." Brow raises his chin and straightens up. "The rest of you can go on ahead, and I'll just camp out here. You can pick me up on your way back."

Jesus Christ.

"You can't seriously think I'm going to leave you alone here for three days," says Michael. "What are you, Robinson fucking Crusoe? I'm sure all those downtown Toronto street smarts will come in real handy when you're panhandling bears. What about shelter?"

Brow shrugs. "Weather's okay for now. And I did a solo like everyone else." He gestures to his sleeping roll. "If I need to, I can always build a lean-to with the rope and plastic."

"You slept out for one goddamn night a ten-minute walk from the main camp. And you came back to the dining hall for breakfast. What will you eat?"

"I'll hunt," he says, holding up one of the cheap Swiss army knife knock-offs he and all the rest of the campers were issued before the trip.

"You'll hunt."

"Yeah."

"Without a licence."

"Ummm . . . Yeah?"

"You're going to camp out for three days, by yourself, and hunt for what, raccoons and squirrels?" Michael's neck and jaw tense. Okay, now he's shouting. And waving his arms. Yet at the same time, he feels curiously disconnected from his own actions, as if he were watching film footage of a complete stranger on the verge of a temper tantrum. With a kid who's been arrested three times for assault. He pauses and forces himself to breathe, to bring his volume back under control. Much better. "So, you figured you'd just hunt. Without a license in Algonquin fucking Park. With nothing but a goddamn jackknife. What are you going to do, wait for animals by a bank machine and mug them? And even if by some miracle you did catch something, it's a goddamn *wilderness conservation area*, for fuck's sake!"

A cluster of canoes passes by on the lake, and Michael is certain they can hear his shouting, but he doesn't care. Brow hunches silently on his rock, looks at the knife still in hand, and glares down at Michael once more, eyes narrowing. Michael glares right back up at him, then slowly bends over, picks up Brow's sleeping roll and turns back towards the canoe.

"Now get down here and help me get this goddamn boat in the water. You take stern." A few long seconds, and Michael hears Brow slide down off the boulder. Footsteps as the boy approaches, then walks past Michael to silently pick up his end of the canoe. But as they manhandle the boat back into the water, Michael catches the tail end of a furtive smirk flitting across the fifteen-year-old's face.

Silently, Michael climbs into the front seat and pushes them out into the shallows. Then he stows his paddle and turns to sit facing his not-quite-AWOL camper. As Brow battles wind and waves for control of the canoe, Michael leans back, hooks his feet up over a thwart, and fishes the Ziplock bag containing his cigarettes from his pocket. He lights up, and the stiff headwind blows each exhaled plume directly into Brow's face. Technically, according to camp rules, neither one of them is allowed to smoke. Unofficially, though, Michael knows that Brow ran out of cigarettes two days ago. And in the entire forty minutes it takes to solo the double-loaded canoe back to the portage, the boy doesn't speak — or smirk — again.

Thanks to Brow's little misadventure, the group doesn't arrive at the new campsite until sunset and is forced to set up camp by flashlight in the rapidly falling dark. By unspoken agreement, Michael and Brow gather firewood while the rest of the campers set up tents. Returning to the firepit, neither speaks aside from the occasional directive, Brow picking out kindling and passing it to Michael, who carefully lays the fire before lighting it with a single match. As the flames spring up, Michael catches Brow's smile of quiet satisfaction in the flickering light and feels the expression echoed on his own face. Later, the two of them sit staring into dwindling coals, everyone else having long since gone to bed. Neither one of them has spoken for quite some time. Michael throws on another branch, offers Brow a cigarette from his diminishing supply, then lights another for himself.

"So uh . . . Sorry I lost it back there."

"It's okay," says Brow.

"Yeah, but still."

"Whatever. The group home staff are way worse." Brow takes another drag on his cigarette, looks off into the darkness. "Some of them will take a kid down for practically nothing. Just slam you down and sit on you. It's how they get their jollies, the sick fuckers."

Michael knows better than to take Brow's testimony at face value. Knows that ninety percent of the time, the restraints he describes as arbitrary are probably entirely necessary. And you can't afford to take that risk with a kid like Brow. Not when you know what could happen the other nine times out of ten. Just one wrong call, and someone could get seriously hurt. So it makes sense the group home workers would err on the side of safety, especially with other kids around. But Michael has also learned the importance of performing trust. Kids lie all the time, but that's not the point. What matters is the subjective experience of being believed. And Michael can give Brow at least that much.

"Yeah, that sounds fucked up," he says.

The six-canoe trailer creaks and sways precariously each time the driver catches one of the deep grooves in the camp laneway, results of a half-summer's worth of rain and erosion. By the time the dusty van crackles to a halt on the gravel in front of the dining hall, a small crowd has gathered to greet the LITs' triumphant return. Michael watches the kids tumble out of the van, that brief moment of disorientation as each one hits the ground and finally realizes that yes, they are right back where they started. The moment passes quickly, replaced by over-boisterous greetings and reassertions of normalcy, rounds of hugs and all the rest.

When Erin rounds the corner of the dining hall, Michael dodges into the crowd and sneaks up behind her, lifting her off her feet with a surprise-attack bear hug. She shrieks, then laughs and bats ineffectively at his shoulders, shrilly and repeatedly ordering him to put her down. When he sets her back on the gravel and tries to steal a kiss, she pushes him away and loudly tells him that he stinks. One of her eight-year-old campers pipes up from behind, echoing her counsellor's assessment: "Eeewww! Stinky!" The girl screws up her face in mock disgust as her cabin-mates burst into gales of laughter. Erin plays along, head tipped back and pinching her nose as she regally waves Michael away. Playing the hulking Barbarian to her demure Princess, Michael hoists Erin over his shoulder, and the girls charge in to the rescue, tugging ineffectively at Erin's legs and Michael's arms. When he finally capitulates and sets Erin back down, she whispers in his ear: "Welcome back, stinky. See you tonight?" Michael smiles, nods briefly, then turns and calls the LITs back from the milling crowd.

Within minutes the fifteen-year-olds are hefting gear and canoes that would have easily bested them only ten days before, and Michael feels a surge of pride at this sudden, collective efficiency. To look at them, you'd never guess just how rare this sort of effortless teamwork had been on the trip. Within half an hour the van and trailer are unloaded, and everyone has scattered to their own personal cleanup, unpacking, and more private return-to-camp rituals. Briefly, Michael wonders how these kids will handle their return to the truly real world of group homes, detention centres, and foster homes, where all the old rules and restrictions will remain entirely unaltered by this supposedly life-changing experience. But the moment passes quickly, vanishing as his thoughts turn to this evening's anticipated reunion.

The next day behind the dining hall, Michael sips his fifth cup of coffee and suppresses a yawn as Tex tells the story of his first successful two-man takedown to a rapt audience of several counsellors on break. Tex is five-foot-nothing and skinny, and genuinely enjoys both his job and the kids he works with. He also knows how to work an audience, which makes him popular with campers and staff alike. Caesar stands towards the back of the crowd, arms crossed and periodically nodding in silent approval. Thirty feet away, Brow practices his juggling. As a part of their leadership training, each LIT had to pick a self-directed learning task, and Brow's choice was juggling pins. He's not very good yet, but the constant practice is beginning to show results, and sometimes he can go for almost a minute before fumbling one.

Tex hops back and forth, bouncing with enthusiasm as he tells the story.

"The kid, he's only twelve, right? But he's *big*. And he's pissed. I mean at first he's just mouthing off at Caesar, but there's no reasoning with him, and he just keeps getting madder and madder. Then he picks up a rake, and he's like, swinging it around and shit. Totally lost it. And I'm like, *damn*, shit just got *real*. I mean, the rest of the kids are backing off fast, but what if he actually hits somebody? 'Cause this isn't some wimpy-ass leaf rake. It's one of those heavy-duty garden ones with *steel teeth*, could do some serious *damage*.

"So I look at Caesar, and he looks at me, and all he says is, 'Let's do this.' And that's it. We square off in front of the kid, and Caesar counts it off . . . One-Two-Three and BOOM." Tex rams the heel of one hand into the palm of the other. "Just like that, the kid's down."

Brow drops a pin, scowls, and retrieves it.

Tex jumps into the air and lands stiff-legged, repeating the hand-thump. "BOOM, and Caesar's on his back, I've got his feet, and that kid can't *move*. Not a *muscle*."

A frown creases Brow's forehead as he tosses the pins higher, sacrificing a degree of control for the extra reaction time.

Tex is riding high on recollected adrenaline, and understandably so. It was a genuinely dangerous situation, no telling how much damage that kid might have done in a crowded space like that. This way, the kid eventually calmed down (facedown in the dirt, he had little choice), and no one was hurt, including him. It worked. It was necessary.

Brow's expression has turned blank, almost meditative, eyes half-focused on a fixed point at the top of the pins' tumbling arcs, and Michael wonders if he too is recalling his own stories of overly enthusiastic group-home workers. After all, the kid with the rake could have just as easily been Brow on a bad day. Maybe it wasn't such a bad thing for Brow to see Michael lose it that day in Algonquin. To know that this counsellor, who had such power over him, was also vulnerable to fits of silly, impotent rage. And to remember that he was the one who remained calm while Michael was the one who lost control.

Erin and Michael spend the first day of the next changeover at Second Point, an isolated peninsula overlooking the lake. Late that night, as he gives Erin a massage in front of the campfire, Michael becomes acutely aware of her lack of a bra, slips his hands under her thin T-shirt, and leans in to kiss her neck, which tastes of suntan lotion. He allows his hands to slide around to her stomach and rise to cup her small breasts, nipples erect against his palms and fingertips as, for the first time, Erin raises her arms and allows him to remove her T-shirt. When she turns to kiss him back, Michael pushes her slowly down to the dew-damp earth, kissing her mouth, neck, and collarbone. Skipping shyly down to her stomach, he slowly works his way up her torso to her breasts, focusing on one and circling slowly inwards, teasing. She inhales sharply and makes small, inarticulate sounds as his movements become more urgent, one hand grasping her from behind as he pulls her into him, his mouth now pressed hard into her stomach. His other hand grips her upper thigh as his lips reach the waist of her jeans.

He feels her tense as he fumbles with the button-fly, his breath turning ragged as she speaks his name — just once, softly. He stops, gasping, and forces himself to rein in this sudden urgency, to relax his grip and take longer, deeper breaths. Slowly, he withdraws, her smooth form laid out before him as she reaches down, still prone and watching him, to re-button her partially opened fly. And in spite of this stopping — or perhaps because of it — this moment feels special, a point of connection. Silently, he absorbs the sight of her watching him watching her, expressionless and intent, a circuit completed.

At the beginning of each session, counsellors receive a sheet with a list of camper names accompanied by cryptic annotations: "B" is Bedwetter, "BP" is Behaviour Problem, "M" is Meds. There's no annotation for Ritalin Holiday, which is too bad, as it would be nice to know in advance when a kid's been forced into withdrawal from their doctor-prescribed speed addiction. Nor is there any notation for Boundary Problems, though both the term and the phenomenon it describes are common enough, referring to kids who have trouble conforming to conventional social boundaries. In some cases they latch on too close, touch too much, compulsively sexualize all of their interactions. Other times, it's just the reverse, and all touch becomes bad touch, all forms of physical affection terrifying. But the craving remains. In the latter instance, some of the smaller ones regularly lash out with strategically ineffective violence, requiring restraint — always a basket hold — on an almost daily basis. In the basket hold, the child's arms are wrapped across the torso and held by the wrists from behind, a knee at the small of the back to keep the child off balance until he or she can be lowered to sit on the ground. The basket hold forces these children to hug themselves.

Other cases are more complex. Like Cory. Fourteen and lanky, a combination of corded, ropy muscle and out-of-control acne, he stinks. A sour, pungent odour easily detectable from several feet away. He never showers, rarely swims, and wears full sweats at all other times: track pants, T-shirt, and hoodie, all black. Thirty degrees in the shade and still he'll be fully covered, hood pulled forward to hide his face from direct sunlight. Cory's got some serious boundary problems and compulsively re-enacts the same scenario with various counsellors.

At first, it seems obscurely flattering. Here's this quiet, awkward kid, hardly ever talks, and he says he feels like he can *really trust you.* He speaks softly, insisting on complete seclusion, explaining that sometimes the other kids and even the staff make him uncomfortable. This is, after all, a part of what you're trying to do. To make a connection. And Cory's a good kid, shy and generally submissive, never causes problems. Maybe, you think, he's coming out of his shell. Except there's this intensity. Eventually he will tell you outright that you are the *only* one he can trust. And as he tells you this, he stares deeply into your eyes, his own dark and liquid, pupils dilated wide. Still speaking, he draws closer and touches you softly on the elbow or shoulder. The touch is intense but not quite sexual, and though there's nothing you can put your finger on, you can *feel* it. He wants something, and he wants it with an intensity analogous to lust. He doesn't just want something from you. He wants *you.*

Most people don't know that Cory killed his parents.

Michael isn't supposed to know this, but he's heard the story through a select and exclusive grapevine. It's hearsay, but from dependable sources. Apparently, he chopped his parents to bits with an axe, a full-on hack job when he was ten or eleven. And from what Michael has heard, he can't bring himself to blame the kid. Cory and his three brothers, one older and two younger, were locked in a dirt-floored garage for their entire childhood.

Clothed in disintegrating rags, they were treated like animals, their primary human contact being when food was tossed in at random intervals through the briefly-opened garage door.

And on an overnight at Second Point, as Cory murmurs to him in the darkness apart from the others, Michael can't help wondering what — if anything — this boy remembers from his childhood. It's a miracle he can interact at all, that he can speak or clothe himself or engage in any pretence of normalcy, no matter how limited. Michael cannot imagine Cory's interiority, and even if he could, he feels he would have no right to do so. All he can do is listen when Cory chooses to talk at times like this, on an overnight campout with two cabins of fourteen-year-old boys, just beyond the glow of a smouldering campfire, the rest of the campers already asleep in their tents. Michael does his best not to flinch when Cory softly touches his elbow and tells him how safe he feels right now.

◊ ◊

The next time Erin says his name that way, they are making out on the rough ground as they have so often before, Erin moving beneath Michael as his hands play over her body beneath her shirt. But this time, something shifts. Michael wedges one leg hard between her thighs and presses upward. Her body presses up against him, thighs tightening around his, fingers digging hard into his upper arm. She says his name, softly, and he presses down, hips moving slowly at first, then faster. She says his name again, louder now, and grips his shoulders tighter yet, those strong hands. And a third time.

"Michael!"

She shouts full-voiced and pushes him off with a sharp upwards surge. For a moment he fully expects her to take control in return, reversing polarities to pin him down and descend as urgently and hungrily upon him as he had upon her.

It takes a few seconds lying there, gasping, before he opens his eyes to find her sitting up, knees pulled into her chest, face hidden by the fall of her hair. She too is breathing hard, but doesn't reach out to touch him, doesn't even glance in his direction. He half-sits and touches her shoulder, but Erin remains utterly still as Michael finally begins to understand what just happened. His initial confusion is followed first by embarrassment at the gracelessness of his actions, dry-humping her leg like a poorly trained dog. Then embarrassment is supplanted by something more like shame, a sudden wave of self-loathing and nausea.

He sits up fully, touches her hair and speaks her name, just once. After a long pause, she raises her head and turns to face him. He strokes her cheek with the back of an index finger. "I'm sorry," he says. He knows this is pathetically inadequate, but he can't think of anything else to say. "Are you all right?"

"I'm fine." A pause. Then Erin shakes her head once, convulsively, as if trying to shake something off — a cobweb or an insect, perhaps.

"Are you sure?"

"I said I'm fine." Sharper this time. A slow, quavering inhalation, and again that head-shake. "Could we just sit for a while? I don't feel like talking right now."

Michael puts a tentative arm around Erin's waist, and she lets him. She lays her head on his shoulder, and he compulsively strokes her hair, listening to the occasional rustle and skitter of invisible wildlife as the two of them stare into the surrounding darkness.

Blink and Michael's differing strengths work well together, which is probably why Jan has kept pairing them with matching male and female cabins all summer. Three sessions in now, they have learned each other's rhythms, developed boiler-plate routines for dealing with everything from bed-wetting to bullying to homesickness. Blink's good with the shy kids, especially the smaller ones, while Michael does best with the bad-asses, enjoying the challenge of staying cool while they try to push his buttons. The two counsellors respect each other's judgement and opinions, even when they disagree, and they have become friends of a sort. Now, as the campers head off to their second activity of the day, Blink and Michael take their hour off together, their respective co-counsellors assuming the task of supervision. Though it's only mid-August, the camp is far enough north that the nights are getting chilly. This early in the morning the breeze is still cool off the lake, so they build a fire in one of the ubiquitous pits. Michael observes aloud that the leaves are starting to change, and the conversation naturally turns to what they'll be doing in the fall. Blink will be moving out of her parents' place for university, where she has been accepted into a social work program. Eventually she hopes to join the RCMP and work in the child welfare division.

That's when she tells Michael about her father. She says it stopped a long time ago, just after she got her period, and she still loves him. She doesn't want to tear the family apart, and if Michael tells anyone, she will deny everything. But she has a younger sister who will be left at home when she moves out. Michael offers no advice, simply listens and asks occasional questions as she works out her plan. She will say nothing to her mother, who in any case didn't believe her last time. Instead, she will visit home often, stay in close contact with her sister, and watch for signs of anything out of the ordinary. If necessary, she will confront her father directly. When she's finished laying out this plan, Michael hugs her and tells her everything's going to be fine. He says he's certain of it. They both know that this is a lie.

When they finish talking, Blink stays behind, tending the dwindling fire as Michael goes directly to the showers. He turns the water as hot as he can stand and cries as quietly as possible in the metal stall. Scalding water strikes needle-points into his back, sluicing off and down the drain. It's a long shower, and by the time Michael emerges his entire body has turned pink and tender, like that of a child.

Now when they make out, all Erin has to do is say Michael's name — just once, flat and quiet. This means *stop now*, and he always does. His name has become her safe word. Or so he hopes. At the end of a long night of talking and chain-smoking, as false-dawn faintly blues the horizon, Erin finally explains why she needs to stop like that. It's not because she's a virgin (although she is), nor because she's a Nice Mennonite Girl (though she is this as well). It's because not so long ago, on a date with a Nice Mennonite Boy she'd been seeing back home, parked and making out on a dark country road, the Nice Mennonite Boy wouldn't stop. By the time she fought him off and got herself out of the car, her underwear was around her knees, and Nice Mennonite Boy was driving away, leaving her to walk the three miles or so to her family's farmhouse alone in the dark. And she never told anyone. Until now.

Now, she says she wants Michael to understand what it means when she says his name like that, but he knows he can't understand. Not really. When she says his name, he stops, and that is enough. Or rather, he thinks with a surge of resentment, it *should* have been enough. She didn't have to tell him *why*, and he finds himself wishing she hadn't. Because the worst part of knowing is that now he can't stop comparing himself to Nice Mennonite Boy. Compulsively, he invents details, the sound of the engine and spitting gravel as he punched the gas and fishtailed away, heart still pounding, to race alone through the dark. The belated realization of what he had (almost) done. Not that he could have been *that* naïve. At some point in the process, he must have known what he was doing. But still. Michael wonders if the Boy knew he had that in him, how he felt the next day. Did he rewrite the story in his mind? Now, Michael worries about those times when he doesn't want to stop, when he can imagine not stopping so *vividly*.

◦ ◦

Next summer, Michael's new girlfriend will be confused by this reflexive stopping.

When she whispers his name while making out, that's not what she means. And when she asks him what's wrong, breathless and offended and maybe even a little hurt, he will find himself entirely unable to explain. He will want to. But he will also know he could never explain such a thing to this tough, beautiful, cynically innocent girl — for whom he is, after all, just another summer fling, nothing more.

THE MYSTERIOUS EAST

(FREDERICTON, NB)

— Seventy-one, on the air.
— Across the top, Seventy-one.
— Right.

Andrew has always loved the kayak for its manoeuvrability, more sensitive and responsive than its loutish cousin the canoe. Some might complain at the relative instability, but he enjoys the challenge. Paddling away from the Small Craft Aquatic Centre, he marvels that this is his first time out on the river. Time was, he would have done this every week. But that was pre-Fredericton, another life. Rocking in the wake of a long-gone motorboat, Andrew instinctively dips his paddle to one side and shifts his weight. The empty bottle clinks against the back of his seat, glass on fibreglass, then rumbles and rolls from side to side against the hull. He twists around to find Jaffee still watching from the parking lot, resting his fat ass against the cab's wheel-well, shading his eyes and squinting to follow Andrew's progress against the glare of sun on water — but already such land-based concerns seem less pressing. Andrew turns forward and puts his back into the paddling, a burst of speed. And though he splashes more than he once would have, the economical stroke of a seasoned kayaker remains.

Rhona didn't give him a time to be back, just sent him out here on this inexplicable errand. The muscles in Andrew's back and arms are warming, a pleasant burn in contrast to the cool river water splashing his hands and forearms, and though the sun is past its zenith, it won't touch the horizon for hours yet. All the time in the world. The rolled-up sleeves of his button-down shirt unroll and dip into the waves every ten or twelve strokes. Like the ten thousand things, they rise and fall without cease, an object lesson in the futility of control. Scattered houses dot the southern bank, and massive concrete bridges loom over the Saint John behind him, but it's easy to ignore those and focus on the soft lapping of water against the hull, the flashing patterns of sunlight on waves, the heavily wooded stretches of the uninhabited north shore ahead. Awash in these physical immediacies, Andrew can almost forget the bottle rattling around back there, Constable Jaffee waiting on shore. Kayaking had always been good for that, a temporary escape being better than none at all.

You'll know it when you see it.

That's what Rhona said, and she hasn't led him wrong yet. Had him on a solid run for three hours and counting, and when your dispatcher sends you off like that, you don't ask questions. You do what you're told, keep that dispatcher as happy as you can, and hope she'll keep the run going. Rhona said to start with the islands, so he points his bow towards the first one and relaxes into the liquid rhythm of his steady, windmilling stroke.

— Fifty-seven. Skyline for a package.
— Right.

Andrew's job interview was short and to the point. The dispatcher on duty verified his cab license, asked about availability, and concluded with an opaque directive: "Pick a number you'll remember."

Andrew picked seventy-one, his birth year, and with that his number was fixed. For the next hour, on early-morning empty streets, another driver showed him how to operate the radio and use a street index. Between six and seven, they took two fares while Andrew learned to always write down his addresses and hand out the proper number of discount tickets. By seven-thirty he was driving solo, his journey of a thousand miles begun. Again.

— Seventy-one, parked at the Regent Mall.
— Right Seventy-one.

In this city, at every moment of every hour of every day, a woman (or a man) sits in a dimly lit room and plays a variant on solitaire with slips of coloured paper for cards, Post-its scrawled with handwritten notes. This person takes a slip from the main stack and places it onto one of several smaller piles scattered across the wooden desk, then presses a button, speaks into a microphone, waits for a response, and nods.

Right, she says, and retrieves the next slip of paper from the main stack, answers the phone if it's ringing. The stacks grow and shrink and occasionally vanish entirely, but the deck is never exhausted. Sometimes, in a brief lull when the phone stops ringing and the radio falls silent, she rolls cigarettes and smokes, the still, dead air growing opaque with thickening clouds.

The players change every eight hours, but the game never does, slips of paper endlessly shuffled around a broad desk. These cards conjure cars to all corners of the city — from darkness, fog, rain, clear daylight — weaving invisible patterns, strands crossing and recrossing the city like nets. Cards for cars, cast across time and space to dip into evanescent schools of passengers, catching them up and taking them wherever it is they think they need to go.

— Thirteen. Two to base.
— Eighteen dollars, Thirteen. Company policy.
— Right.

Andrew's first fare was a writer whose day job was the night-shift at Cendant, a local call centre based in a dying mall on the Northside and dealing with worldwide car rentals. (When looking for work, Andrew had drawn the line just this side of a call centre job, the only other sure-fire employment in this town if you didn't work for the government or the University.) The guy said he hated the place, all the people he worked with, and every single idiotic customer he'd ever talked to. He never showed anyone what he wrote, though. He didn't want them to get the wrong impression, what with all the graphic, extended torture scenes incorporating his co-workers and assorted call centre clientele.

"I mean, you've got to write what you know, right? But it's all, like, imaginary. Nothing autobiographical. 'Cause that'd be, like, seriously fucked up. Still, gotta put all that pent up frustration somewhere, right?"

"So once you've written it out, does that mean you're not frustrated any more?"

"Not really, no."

That first day, Andrew made fifty dollars for a twelve-hour shift: four dollars and seventeen cents an hour. To celebrate, he bought bagels, instant noodles, eggs, coffee, and a pack of smokes. Rent could wait at least another week. *The sage stays behind, thus he is ahead.*

⁙

— Thirteen. Got the dough and on the go.
— Right Thirteen. Let me know when you're back.

⁙

Andrew explores the chain of islands strung out along the north shore, paddling in close and watching, learning the rhythm and pattern of this space so he can spot anything out of the ordinary. Whatever clue or sign Rhona expects him to recognize. Some islands are so long and close to the riverbank that he second-guesses his choice of routes, half expecting the narrow passages to dead end in a shallow bay before he reaches the far side. Others rise in regular chains of grassy hillocks, rows of perfectly round humps no more than twenty or thirty feet across, their spacing so geometrically precise it seems hardly possible for them to have formed naturally. As if some obscure and deeply Canadian sea-serpent was caught and trapped here in a sudden hard freeze, slowly starving to death over the winter months to leave only this ossified and decomposing carcass as a remembrance. Long grasses springing up over centuries to mask and reclaim its ancient, waterlogged flesh.

— Seventy-one, 48 Abbot Court.
— Right.

His second day started slow, and Andrew was tired, so he drank coffee to stay awake: three extra-large triple-triples in the first two hours. Later, when a sudden flurry of calls arrived with no chance for a break, he came close to pissing himself right there in the front seat. And though the sage pointed out that the great Tao flows everywhere, exhorting his followers to be the stream of the universe, Andrew was pretty sure this wasn't what he had meant. Eventually, he pulled over in an apartment parking lot on his way to a call and went against the side of the building, the volume on his radio turned up to maximum in case he got yet another call while he was out. Not until he was zipped up and climbing back into the cab did Andrew notice the open basement apartment window, right next to the foaming urine stream rapidly soaking into parched gravel. But by the end of the day, no one had complained, and he hadn't missed any calls. Andrew considered himself lucky and learned from the experience.

That day, he made sixty-two dollars and fifteen cents.

— Forty-two, got my gas and coming in.
— Right Forty-two.
— Gonna grab a coffee on the way. Anyone want anything up there?
— Yeah, just hang on. *[A lengthy pause.]* One medium double-triple, two extra-large triple-triples, and a large tea with milk.
— Right.

This room could be almost anywhere, and several like it are scattered throughout the city. There are no windows, and the only furniture consists of a desk, two squeaky wooden swivel chairs, a telephone, and a microphone. On the bulletin-board over the desk hangs a map of the city, dusted with red and blue push-pins, marked off with taxi-stands, discount rates, and fare-zones. In such a room, in the conjunction of zone-map, phone, microphone, and shuffling slips of paper, a person might learn to read and understand the language of the city, to map the arcane whisperings of its structural dreams. The ten thousand things, rising and falling. A dispatcher dreaming a butterfly dreaming a city dreaming a dispatcher.

— Seventy-one, one to Cendant.
— Seven-fifty, Seventy-one.
— Right.

At first when Andrew's fares asked about his background, he tried to be as honest as possible. Within limits. He told them he'd left his job as a personal service representative at a Waterloo insurance company to move out east where the pace of life was slower, the cost of living less. Kind of a post-9/11 thing, like that lawyer who quit his corporate job to become a Starbucks barista. He'd considered moving west, but though he liked pot as much as the next guy, it had just seemed so clichéd. Everyone and his dog moved out west at some point or another, and even those who didn't come back in a year or two with their tails between their legs said rent in Vancouver was a bitch.

But some of his regulars wanted more, with follow-up questions that were simultaneously tedious and invasive. Why here instead of Halifax? Any family back in Ontario? What about girlfriends? So Andrew started inventing different backstories for the more inquisitive ones. He might be a physics graduate student, a former corporate lawyer, a struggling artist, an ex-con. The challenge was to keep track of which fare had heard which story so he could continue it seamlessly the next time he picked them up. To keep the story going and make it real. To mimic sincerity so well that sometimes he almost believed it himself.

* *

— Ninety-nine approaching.
— You hold off there a minute, Ninety-nine. Might have something for you.
— Right.

* *

Expecting the sudden scurry of wildlife, Andrew doesn't notice the cattle until he's almost passed them by. They lie so still in the long grass that he has to look twice to be sure he hasn't imagined them, chewing their cud and following his progress with bored, half-lidded eyes. Emblems of perfect wisdom, they abide in non-action (*yet nothing is left undone*). Perhaps a dozen lie scattered within a few hundred feet, each with a bright yellow plastic tag affixed to its left ear.

Andrew has heard of these cattle on the islands of the Saint John River, which provide ideal summer pasturage. The grass is plentiful, and most of the islands are partially wooded, so there's no shortage of shade. As for water, no drought has ever dried up this river. Cattle don't swim, so the only danger of losing them would be through poaching — or would that be "rustling"? (Andrew has a brief, bizarre vision of swash-buckling river-buccaneers in dungarees and cowboy hats, rustling cattle on the high seas.) In the spring, riverfront farmers simply take their herds over to a convenient island and leave them there. And each fall, when the temperature drops and snow flies they retrieve and pack them away in landlocked barns.

And yet, confronting these incongruous transplanted beasts in the flesh, Andrew finds that they radiate an air of propri-etary ease, as if they have emerged whole from the earth on this very spot, outgrowths of the island itself. Their absurd-ity is its own sanction, reminding him of a conversation he once had with a guy whose family has been here since the seventeenth century. He asked where Andrew was from, and when Andrew answered offhandedly, "Here now, I guess," the formerly friendly guy responded with instant dead-eyed conviction: *You will never be from here.* Andrew drifts, paddle stowed and balanced across the deck as the largest cow raises her head, flips an ear, and eyes him as if to challenge his sur-prise at her presence. As if to say, "*We* have always been here. *You* are the interloper."

— Seventy-one, clear.

— Right Seventy-one. Come on back.

— Right.

"So I got two doubles and a triple out to Gagetown Base, six military bucks an' a chick. Good load, right? Even at closing time. 'Cept halfway out, two young guys start gettin' into it over dis chick, who's gonna take her home an' shit."

Twenty-three steered the van with one hand and gesticulated wildly with the other as she drove Andrew home from his shift.

"Older guys, dey said, 'Yeah, we know dis cunt, always talkin' like dat, stirring up shit, startin' fights.' So I told de young bucks, ignore de cunt. An' I told de cunt to shut her fuckin' mouth or I'd drop her right dere and fuck de money. Shut up or walk home an'at's all dere was to it. I got dat cunt outta dere right quick, I tell you. No goddamn fights in my cab."

Andrew learned a lot about cabbie culture by listening to the other drivers. Not from the anecdotes themselves but from incidental details. Patterns of recurrent phrases and repetitions, hints of unspoken, implicit knowledge. From Twenty-three, he learned that your best bet at closing time (especially in a van) was to hang around the bars and stuff that van to the gills for a series of short runs with multiple drop-offs. Ten, fifteen minutes tops for the run, then you could head back and do it all over again, milking that golden hour from two to three for all it was worth. But every now and then, a full load could make a Base run worth your while. Two doubles and a triple — three full fares plus a dollar apiece for the extras — would make you sixty-one bucks plus tip on a fifty-minute round trip. Even better if you caught a return fare, but you couldn't count on that.

From Fifty-seven, Andrew learned about local politicians' back-room deals, as well as a more speculative network of conspiracies spiralling out from the central figure of President George Dubyah. "You want to know what's really going on, ask a cabbie," he'd say with a wink and a tap alongside his nose. "We see things." From Forty-two, Andrew learned the fine art of *chiselling*, the practice of ripping off the owners by strategically misreporting fares. You had to be careful, but every so often you could take an extra fare or two and pocket the cash rather than settling for the usual forty-percent commission. The trick was not to wander too far from your last reported location so as to avoid getting caught off guard by an unexpected call. As Forty-two put it, "You're not a real cabbie if you don't chisel enough for food and smokes."

By this measure, Andrew has never been a real cabbie. Not because he was afraid of the consequences of being caught. So far as he could tell, chiselling was pretty much an open secret, and the worst that ever happened was a few missed shifts and being forced to pay back the cash. Slap on the wrist, really. But the mere idea of getting caught made his stomach churn — not with fear, but with anger. The sheer indignity of it, getting caught scamming for an extra couple of bucks as if it would make that much difference. Which it would.

— Seventy-one, approaching the bridge.
— Right, Seventy-one. You come on over and head to the liquor store.
— Right.
— And when you get there, Seventy-one, you go on in and pick up a bottle of Prince Igor. Let me know when you're back.
— Right.

A dispatcher might learn the city like a body, cars and people flowing like blood down arterial roadways, up and down the hill on Regent and Smythe, across the Princess Margaret and Westmoreland bridges to the Northside and back. Walmart a pulsing commercial heart pumping cash and cheap goods both into and out of the semi-urban provincial capital.

Up Regent, the five o'clock rush lasts twenty-five minutes, and a misdirected cab can take that whole time to travel the seven sluggish blocks from Dundonald to Prospect. But with a tiny nudge or the smallest delay, a good dispatcher (with well-seasoned drivers) can perform urban bypass surgery at rush half-hour, diagnosing the slightest of hitches in that constant, pulsing beat.

— Seventy-one.
— Go ahead, Seventy-one.
— I'm back. Got the bottle.
— Right Seventy-one. Why don't you hang out downtown for a bit? Just find yourself a spot and hang tight. Lots up top right now.
— Right.

And the blowjobs. Andrew never once saw or heard of anyone going down on a girl in the back of a cab, but the blowjobs were ridiculous. Drunken couples, bar pick-ups, and the occasional hooker — no one seemed to give it a second thought. Andrew had thought the other drivers were bullshitting him until the day he started his shift two hours early. Four o'clock in the morning, he was half-asleep and undercaffeinated, driving a young couple home from a party. Both were messy drunk, slightly overweight, pasty white twenty-somethings in the usual uniform: him in jeans, T-shirt, and a baseball cap; her flashing the obligatory thong between low-rise jeans and a too-tight party shirt. When Andrew glanced in the mirror and saw the girl's head bobbing in the guy's lap, a flash of pasty white hip (his) not quite hidden by the fall of her hair, he resolved not to look back again. But having once glimpsed it, he found it impossible to ignore. It sounded like a greedy child eating pudding, and it went on and on and on.

When he finally said something, the girl simply raised her head, wiped her mouth, and absentmindedly continued stroking the guy with one hand as she turned to face Andrew. The guy, eyes closed and face slack with booze and arousal, moaned in protest at the interruption.

"It's okay, mister," she said. "I swallow. No mess or nothing."

"That's not the point," said Andrew.

The guy looked like he might have passed out, head lolled off to one side and erection waning, but when the girl returned to her ministrations he seemed to perk up soon enough. Andrew considered stopping and kicking them out right there, but didn't. Instead, he turned up the radio and tried to keep his eyes on the road. The one time Andrew glanced in the rearview mirror, the guy smiled as he caught Andrew's glance, holding it for a slightly too-long second. Then he moaned — a soft sound entirely at odds with that lightly amused grin — tapped the side of his nose, and winked.

Andrew didn't look back again.

● ●

— Seventy-one, you parked yet?

— Nope, not yet. Taxi-stands are all full.

— Just park up ahead on your right, Seventy-one. Next empty spot.

— Right.

Beaching his kayak on the boggy, uncertain shoreline, Andrew jams his paddle into the mud for balance and wiggles his way out of the cockpit. By the time he makes it up onto shore, his cotton pants are drenched and muddy to the knees, the ankle-deep water having given way to a foot of mud beneath. Under the impassive eye of the cow he thinks of as the matriarch, he slides the kayak into the long grass, where it will be invisible from the water.

Andrew retrieves the vodka bottle from behind the seat and slowly approaches the matriarch, bottle in one hand, the other empty and held forward, palm up and towards her nose. When he's a foot away, she huffs once but remains still. Her massive black, brown, and white bulk makes him feel insignificant, his posture transforming him into a supplicant before the bored queen. As he lays a hand on her side, he imagines that any boredom so implacable must be a sign of either great wisdom or colossal stupidity. He wonders what she would say if she could speak. She might indignantly order him off her island or explain with immense pride how she and her clan have lived here for generations. She might challenge him with riddles.

Or her broad flank might twitch under his open palm, the short, coarse hair vibrating for a moment, then stopping. She might turn that massive head aside, press the bridge of her nose against his hip, and give him a single, solid nudge towards the low-hanging branches a little farther down-shore. As if to say, *Over there. Try looking over there.*

Andrew removes his hand from the warm flesh and picks his way around the cow-patties and towards the smaller, shadowed shapes barely visible through the trees.

— Seventy-one, parked at Reid's newsstand.
— Right Seventy-one. You see that dog tied to the fire hydrant?
— Wiener dog out front of Coffee Revolution?
— That's the one. Get out, pet that dog, and let me know when you're back.
— Right.

Night-driving had its own rhythm, steady at first, then the bar-closing rush followed by the typically long and empty hours until morning. So Andrew was relieved when he got a call to the Beaverbrook Hotel at three thirty. The woman, who looked to be in her early forties, climbed into the van, gave him a Northside address, lit a cigarette and took a drag, then asked if he minded. By way of an answer, he rolled down the windows and lit one up himself, then listened and nodded occasionally as she talked and talked and talked.

She said it was strange to be back after so long away, and she'd been working non-stop since her return, trying to get the business back up and running. It was hard to find the right kind of girls in this town, and besides, a lot of her old customers were picky that way and wanted her exclusively. She'd brought in a few girls from Moncton, but they had more enthusiasm than ability, and she had a reputation to uphold. Then again, the Moncton girls had come with a recommendation, which meant she had to at least give them a chance. Just

151

not with the regulars, which was why she was so exhausted right now. Three days straight with hardly any sleep at all, she needed a break.

The woman's cigarette had burned down as she talked, and she tapped the column of ash onto the floor before taking another good long drag. She knew most of the older drivers by name and asked about a few, but Andrew only knew them by number. She asked Andrew if he was new, and when he admitted he'd only been driving for a few months, she said that explained everything. "Don't you worry, honey," she said. "I'll take good care of you." Then she pulled out a cell phone and started dialling. Andrew zoned out as he crossed the Westmoreland bridge and negotiated the warren of unfamiliar back streets while the woman—true to her word—paused occasionally in her running conversation to give him directions through a series of narrow one-way streets lined with vacant shops and cut-rate rooming houses. From one-sided snippets of conversation, he gathered she was talking to a friend at their destination and wondering who might be up at this time of night.

"Okay, I'll be up in a minute," she said as they pulled into the driveway of a rundown tenement with several boarded-up windows. Then she hung up and asked Andrew to wait while she went inside. She emerged with a hard-bitten little guy in jeans, a jean-jacket, and a mesh-back baseball cap. They climbed into the back of the van and, in the pauses between the woman's increasingly frustrated phone calls, discussed who might have some. Giving Andrew a series of in-town addresses, they changed their minds several times before the little guy got fed up, produced the sixty dollars up-front for an hour rental, and directed Andrew out to a place he called the Clubhouse. The address he gave was twenty minutes out of town to the north, just past the Marysville bridge, and Andrew glanced at the woman for confirmation. She shrugged her agreement, and Andrew called it in.

They all smoked as Andrew negotiated the winding dark road, and the woman introduced her friend as one of the richest men in Fredericton. "Didn't even finish high school, but you ask anyone who knows and they'll tell you he runs this town." The guy smiled and nodded to Andrew as he ashed his cigarette onto the floor. "And he's the *best* guy, too. You're a real nice guy, aren't you?" The guy nodded again, then when she turned away (still extolling her friend's many virtues) he winked at Andrew, still smiling. Andrew didn't find this comforting. The Clubhouse turned out to be a small grey building at the end of an unlit gravel laneway. More than anything, it looked like a two-room motel with no office, the lane widening out into parking spots for two rooms with matching grey plywood doors.

The little guy and the woman went inside, and the woman emerged alone ten minutes later, cradling a crumpled brown paper bag to her chest as if afraid someone might snatch it away at any moment. As she climbed in, she whispered an address out the Hanwell Road on the far side of town, then fell silent. She chain-smoked and stared out the front window, where the road coalesced from nothing in the van's headlights, curves appearing in the windshield like a video game before vanishing into the pitch blackness out the side and rear windows. Andrew found the silence restful. The van interior was lit only by the blue glow of the dashboard and the winking red cherries of their cigarettes.

Partway into town something bounded onto the road, emerging from the steep slope down to the river on the left. Half the size of the van, the full-grown buck seemed to float for a moment in the headlights, frozen at the peak of its arc. Andrew was transfixed by the sight of it, this massive yet seemingly weightless animal bearing down on them at eighty kilometres an hour. He had enough time to guess the number of points on that rack (twelve at least) but his foot hadn't even touched the brakes by the time the moment passed, the deer touching down briefly on the yellow line before rebounding up the steep and heavily wooded slope to the right. Neither Andrew nor the woman spoke, and the rest of the drive passed in silence.

— Seventy-one. I'm back and . . . ummm . . .
— Go ahead, Seventy-one.
— Drunk on the street here says he's got a message for you.
— You got a pen and paper?
— Already wrote it down.
— Good man, Seventy-one.
— You want it now?
— Not on the radio, Seventy-one. You got that Prince Igor handy?
— Right here in my hot little hands.
— Good. Now here's what you're going to do. You open that bottle, keep the cap, and swap your full Prince Igor for his empty one. Once you've done that, fold up the message, put it in the empty bottle, and screw the cap back on there good and tight. You got all that?
— Swap the bottles, keep the cap, message in the empty, seal it up tight.
— Right Seventy-one. You do that, then hold up there and I'll get back to you.
— Right.

After a certain amount of driving, the car becomes an extension of the body, the driver *becoming* the car. Just so, a dispatcher might *become* an entire fleet, developing a kinaesthetic awareness of each vehicle's position, knowing it as one knows the position of one's own body even with eyes closed. But for the mystically inclined, a refined awareness of the body and its processes is only the first step. The next is learning to control the autonomic systems more consciously: breathing, pulse, brain waves. For focus, a mantra may be of some use, repeated to the point of nonsense and beyond, to the immanent something-from-nothingness of a Zen koan. The dispatcher's mantra consists of the simplest of syllables: *Right.*

Over time, a dispatcher might learn to use the fleet as a means of extending beyond the merely human range of a single, localized consciousness. And this extended being might learn to perceive and communicate with other extended, non-localized entities, to communicate directly with the consciousness of the city itself. A series of discrete actions, taken in the proper order, incomprehensible in isolation yet adding up to *something*. Such a dispatcher might become something more than a person. And such a being might perform occasional miracles, handing them out like koans to particularly favoured drivers.

— Seventy-one! You gettin' bored yet?
— Now how could I get bored with all this stimulating conversation?
— *[laughter]* Right Seventy-one. Got something for you, so listen up.
— Right.
— You take your bottle, head out the PM, and stop at the second piling out. Just stop right there, put on your four-ways, and chuck that bottle hard as you can over the side.
— Princess Margaret, second piling out. Chuck the bottle. East side of the bridge?
— Right Seventy-one.
— Right.

A good dispatcher could make all the difference. A solid run with a pick-up near every drop off, keep you going all afternoon and net you more money in five hours than you might otherwise make in a full twelve-hour shift. Long as you didn't piss off your dispatcher, you were sitting pretty. But sometimes a dispatcher could be so good it was downright creepy, knowing Andrew's location better than he did himself, fares conjuring themselves from thin air at just the right spot, the right time. Like that one afternoon driving down the hill.

— Seventy-one, turn left. Second driveway on your left, right *now.*

The Hanwell was bumper to bumper all the way down, but at that precise moment a perfect gap in traffic appeared in front of the empty driveway. Andrew didn't think about it, just took the opportunity and turned. Almost before he'd stopped moving, the fare was climbing in and giving him an address. Then he caught another perfect gap to head back up, and off he went. Not until hours later, looking over his jotted list of fares, did Andrew realize he had never received a starting address for that call.

— Seventy-one.
— Go ahead, Seventy-one.
— Gonna be a little while here. Got pulled over.
— *[muffled swearing]* Where's the bottle?
— Under the seat.
— Where you at?
— Piling and a half out on the PM bridge.
— Right Seventy-one. You sit tight and let me know if any thing changes.
— Right.

It's cooler and darker under the trees, grass giving way to damp bare earth. As Andrew's eyes adjust, the four dark mounds in front of him resolve into more resting cattle, these ones facing the edge of the trees like sentries. Ahead and down a slight slope, several smaller shapes mill about in the gloom. The only sound is a slight clinking, accompanied by the rippling swish of disturbed water. Andrew descends the slope to the edge of a dark pool, the smaller shapes revealing themselves as wading calves, and again he hears that clinking. He steps into the water, which is shockingly cold. The calves shuffle nervously and retreat to the far side, about twenty feet away. Something hard and smooth bumps his knee, and he scoops it from the water with his free hand: a bottle identical to the one he already carries, Prince Igor vodka, drained and capped, with a scrap of yellow inside.

Eyes fully adjusting, Andrew now sees dozens of identical floating bottles bobbing and colliding in the wake of the calves' retreat. He returns to the edge of the pool and pushes the base of his bottle into the soft earth further up the bank, then uncaps the one he just retrieved from the water and upends it over his open palm. A folded piece of lined yellow paper falls out. He considers unfolding it to read its contents, but he knows this message isn't for him. In the end he drops the still-folded paper back into the bottle, replaces the plastic cap, and turns back to drop the bottle into the water, where it drifts slowly back into the shifting, clinking mass. He wonders what secret currents govern these bottles' movements, what hidden springs.

Returning to claim the original bottle, he finds a brown paper bag in its place. It's curiously dry for such a damp space, and not a speck of dirt clings to its underside as he lifts it up. The bag is so light it could be empty, and it looks exactly like

the one the woman carried as she emerged from the Clubhouse
that night of the deer. He didn't know what was in that bag
then, and he doesn't need to know what's in this one now. *You'll
know it when you see it*, Rhona said. And he does, with a certainty beyond words, beyond reason. He also knows what he
has to do now. Clutching the paper bag to his chest, he glances
one last time at the dark pool, floating bottles, milling calves.
Then he stands, turns his back on all of them, and leaves.

— Seventy-one. You still waiting?
— Yeah, he's running the license and registration.
— Can you see the plate on that cop car?
— GQA 924.
— Right. I'll get back to you.

When Andrew got the call barely two minutes into his shift,
just past six in the morning, it seemed like a promising start to
the day. Then he waited for ten minutes outside the rundown
house with peeling clapboard siding. He was about to give up
when a girl came out. She wore a high-slit backless dress of
some shiny, silky material that draped and clung in such a way
as to give an overpowering impression of *slippery*. She could
have been anywhere from fifteen to twenty-five. The girl got
in the front seat, gave Andrew an address well outside of town,
then smiled and stared off into space as he put the cab in gear
and started driving. After a few minutes of silence, she spoke
dreamily, still staring out the window.

"Do you love Beck's?"

"Sorry?"

"Beck's. It's beer," she said, turning that smile on Andrew.

"I love Beck's." As he racked his brain for an appropriate response, he wondered what she was on.

"Yeah, it's okay."

"Beck's is the best." She sighed, eyes losing focus then returning to a spot just above Andrew's head. "What's that?" She pointed to Andrew's taxi licence, tucked into the sun visor.

"It's my, uh, my taxi license." Andrew wished he was more awake. "Got to keep it where people can see it, or I could get a fifty dollar fine. From a bylaw officer, I mean. If they didn't see it." Andrew kept his eyes on the road and tried to concentrate on driving.

"Can I see it?"

He took the license down and handed it over. She held it up to the light, squinting a little, then handed it back. "That's a great picture. Very hot." Andrew felt himself blushing as he replaced the card in its transparent sleeve and the girl continued asking about everything from the details of the car (yes, it was a refurbished police cruiser) to Andrew's personal grooming (no, he cut his own hair at home) to his usual choice of beer (Picaroons, lately). "Hot," she said, to every response. Judging by the girl's over-generous assessment of pretty much everything — the taxi-licence photo, for example, was a tiny, low-resolution black and white head shot, grainy enough to erase Andrew's multiple piercings and turn his features unflatteringly round and innocent — he was guessing pot, or ecstasy at the very most.

Their destination was an antiseptically middle-class split-level with a manicured lawn, double garage, and a brightly painted metal swing-set visible in the back yard. When they pulled into the driveway, the girl paused in her chatter and turned to face him directly. He revised his age estimate downwards as she smiled, bit her lip, and leaned forward, eyes cast demurely down, the cowl-neck of her dress falling away from her collarbone.

"That'll be eight-fifty," said Andrew, examining the part in her hair, which was very, very straight. She looked up, and the eyes that caught his were somewhere between pale blue and grey, pupils dilated wide. He wondered if she wore colour contacts to get that startling contrast of light eyes and dark hair. Then she leaned in closer and whispered in his ear.

"I don't have any money."

At the end of his shift, Andrew told the other drivers the bizarre story, emphasizing his complete incredulity at being offered a blowjob for a fare. When the other drivers laughed and slapped him on the back, he blushed and laughed uncomfortably along. Twenty-three made several crude jokes, Thirteen asked for the address, and Ninety-nine asked for the girl's number. Fifty-seven, a Christian, scowled and said nothing. Forty-two ignored the rest of them, solemnly placed a hand on Andrew's shoulder, looked him in the eye, and said, "*Now* you're a real cabbie."

Rhona just laughed and laughed and laughed.

— All right, Seventy-one, why don't you tell me what Constable Jaffee's doing right now?

— Constable Jaffee?

— The cop.

— Oh, right. He's back in the cruiser, turned the flashers off, and he's waving at me.

— Right. Change of plan, Seventy-one. Jaffee's going to block traffic while you turn around, then he's going to follow you back across the bridge. No need to get freaked out, now. He's just providing an escort.

— Right.

— So now you're heading to the Small Craft Aquatic Centre. You know where that is?

— Yeah, I know it.

— Good, Seventy-one. You head on over then.

— Right.

A smart driver never questions his dispatcher except to ask for necessary clarification. And dispatchers do not explain themselves. Ever. The red blood cell doesn't need to know why it's carrying oxygen to a particular destination, merely that it must. A driver might search for meaning in his calls, might wonder if some hidden purpose guides these apparently random, discrete tasks. And on the very rarest of occasions, an astute driver might catch the slightest glimmer, some hint of a pattern.

— Seventy-one?

— *[pause]* Go ahead, Seventy-one.

— I'm at the Small Craft Aquatic Centre, in the parking lot.

— Right Seventy-one. You hop out, see if they've got any kayaks available for the next few hours, and let me know. .

— Right.

Recently, on days off, Andrew has taken to cycling out to the booster station along one of the bike trails that riddle the countryside like intestinal parasites. He's been learning to appreciate the joys of human-powered locomotion, a welcome escape from the mechanized routine of always driving, driving, driving. The other day, on his way there, he startled a young deer. Watching it bound off between the trees, he felt a brief moment of kinship, the two of them ghosting through the same woods, free of the town and its incessant machine-driven racket.

Andrew didn't know what a "booster station" was — something to do with the municipal water system, maybe — but that's what the brass plaque said, mounted on the small brick building at the end of his thirty-minute ride out from town. Past the booster station, the woods opened out into a broad clearing hedged in on all sides by tall pines, the only access points being the gravel bike trail and a narrow laneway at the far end. Mounds of rubble filled the space, maybe a dozen or more: gravel, asphalt, and concrete piled up to fifteen feet, nearly half the height of the surrounding trees. The mounds dwarfed the merely human observer and gave the whole space a vaguely post-apocalyptic feel, like an elephant graveyard but for parking lots.

Lately, Andrew has gone there often, drawn by the silence, the occasional deer, those eloquently inarticulate mounds of rubble surrounded by tall trees. Something he cannot name.

— Seventy-one?
— Go ahead, Seventy-one.
— Yeah, they've got a kayak free. Fourteen bucks an hour, no limit.
— Perfect, Seventy-one. So here's what you're going to do.

Emerging from the trees, Andrew is blinded for a moment by the slanting light of the setting sun. Shading his eyes, he walks past the cattle and waves to the matriarch, who flips a bored ear in farewell. He retrieves the kayak from its hiding place, pushes it bow-first into the water, and transfers the paper bag from hands to teeth so as not to get it wet. Then he sits with a leg on either side of the kayak, paddle crosswise behind him for balance, slides on his ass out the deck, and carefully lowers himself into the cockpit. Almost, he dumps it, but not quite. He places the bag in his lap, points the kayak towards open water, and starts paddling. With the rattle of bottle on hull gone, the relative silence of wind and wave deepens. He rounds the end of the island, orients himself, and points his bow towards downtown Fredericton, where his cab — and Constable Jaffee — await. Then he stops. Just stops, stows his paddle, and waits. Trusting the current to take him wherever it is he needs to go.

THE SMUT STORY (I)

A NOTE ON THE (MISSING) TEXT(S) [1]

*This story is not for reading, but for telling. Not for you,
but for your lover.*

*This is the story of a story of a story. If it happens
to turn you on, that is nothing more than a side effect.
Like sex, it can take a thousand different forms, but it
always progresses through a narrative: beginning, middle,
end (... and end ... and end ...). As much as you might
wish it — and you often do — no single instance can go on
forever. This story is collaborative. You tell it with as well
as to your lover. And always, the story starts not with your
lover, but with you.*

It is, after all, your story.

---

1 Excerpted from Dr. Maria Quinlan's introduction to the 2059 edition of
The Smut Story: Critical Reflections (Vanitate Books), released in honour
of the (alleged) fiftieth anniversary of the Mother's Day Affair.

Thus begins — and ends — the only verifiable surviving fragment of "(The Importance Of) Being One's Own Pornographer," as performed by the mysterious Tio Boop.[2] Whether or not one believes that this performance ever happened, its seminal (or perhaps ovarian) influence on Eva S's work remains undeniable.[3] Boop's inexhaustible (and by all accounts unforgettable) story haunts the study of Eva S's work at every turn, echoing down the decades to reverberate in every scholarly paper, every ethnographic study of Eva S fandom, and every Eva S performance. Even so, in producing the first edition of this volume, my co-editors and I agreed that it would be best to omit any transcriptions of Tio Boop's original story, acknowledging its central importance only through the title.[4]

2 This passage is technically "verifiable" only in the sense that it is the sole fragment of Tio Boop's story to remain consistent across all versions and to have been both endorsed and circulated by Eva S. However, the original source of this fragment remains a matter of significant scholarly dispute.

3 While many believe that Eva S has empirically verified the contents of the Boop passage cited above through her ongoing collection of first-hand accounts from the original reading, others argue that she may have invented the "collection" itself (at least initially) in an attempt to imagine what attendees might have heard and what such accounts might have sounded like, had any existed. Still others contend that the Eighteen Year Letter, Tio Boop, and even the Mother's Day Affair itself are nothing more than an elaborate hoax (or performance piece) designed to mythologize Eva S's critical engagement with her own artistic practice and philosophy. However, neither I nor my former co-editors subscribe to any of these overly elaborate theories, preferring instead to take Ms. S at her word.

4 Although they have declined to append their names to this edition, I must thank Doctors Linda Martin and John Torres, co-editors of the original 2044 edition of *The Smut Story*, for their contributions to the text. I still believe that our differing perspectives — and occasionally vigorous debates — ultimately made this volume the success it has been for the past fifteen years. Nonetheless, we all agreed then, as I believe now, that referencing "The Smut Story" — the colloquial term by which Smutsters the world over now refer to Tio Boop's original story — in the title constituted the perfect acknowledgement of Ms. (or Mr.) Boop's contribution both to Eva's work and to this volume.

And although I have expanded this edition with several more recent critical reconsiderations of Eva S's oeuvre, I still stand by that decision.

Certainly, numerous "transcriptions" of Boop's story are available from both online and print sources, and though the contents vary wildly, each one opens with the passage quoted above and echoes the underlying structure described in Hermen's 2010 press conference.[5] However, the most reliable versions of Boop's story remain accessible only through Eva S's extensive audio archive of first-hand oral accounts of the original reading.[6] As the self-appointed guardian and archivist of the Smut Story — which she often cites as the primary inspiration for her own career as an erotic performance artist[7]

---

5 Like the original reading, the events of the Hermen press conference cannot be verified via the public record, although all of the organizers named in the (alleged) press conference transcript agree that it is accurate insofar as they can recall. Indeed, to date, the only "verified" attendees to either the original Mother's Day Affair or the subsequent press conference are the Hermen organizers themselves, since even second-hand published accounts — such as those the aforementioned transcript attributes to "Peter Smith" — have been lost, presumably erased by the info-liberationist (or, according to some, info-terrorist) group known only as "We."

6 Eva S has been collecting these stories for decades, having issued a call in 2030 (which remains open) for anyone who remembers Tio Boop's original performance to visit the archive in person and recite his (or her) story in its entirety. These recitations are recorded directly to audio files, thus preserving the precise nuance, intonation, and rhythm of each storyteller's voice, which Eva S maintains is an utterly crucial aspect of the project.

7 Eva S's iconic breakout performance piece, "Fuck(ing) the Pope" (2029), has remained available online since its original (unauthorized) filming, the posting of which prompted an immediate firestorm of debate that has been well-documented elsewhere. (For insightful discussion of the shifting social and moral anxieties attached to these debates by various groups in the fifteen years following the video's release, see Sharon Riddle's "'Blasphemy,' 'Obscenity,' 'Pornography,' and 'Art' as (Sub)Cultural Diagnostics: Mapping 'Moral' Readings of Eva S's 'Fuck(ing) the Pope' from 2029 to 2044.") To date, Eva has declined to comment on whether the sex

— Ms. S strictly regulates access to these recordings, keeping them available to the public on two conditions: (1) that no recording devices may be used to reproduce or transmit these stories beyond the archive,[8] and (2) that no one may listen to these recordings in solitude but must be accompanied by at least one companion with whom they will discuss the story

---

and orgasms were real or simulated, or whether the recorded audience reactions were spontaneous or a scripted part of the performance. The priest in this video has long since been identified (and defrocked) and has likewise declined to comment on the real or simulated nature of his own participation. Eva's career since then — from the early live performances to her later audio sculptures, which range from the conceptual ("Fidelity," 2047) to the ironically pornographic ("Seventies Bush," 2048) — has likewise been well-documented in both popular media and a variety of scholarly publications. For further reading on Eva S's artistic trajectory from internet porn sensation to subcultural icon to internationally respected performance artist, see Jonathan Torres' landmark critical monograph, *Pornography and/as Art: The Rise of a Reluctant Icon* (2049).

8 Accessed by a gravel laneway, Eva S's estate consists of an aging two-storey farmhouse on a half-acre lot with a spacious garden, several fruit-bearing trees, and a broad, well-kept lawn. No fences or other obvious external security systems distinguish the home from any others in the area, and the archive is housed in a modest addition out back. However, while the estate is open to physical visitors, it is a technological fortress. All virtual intrusions — from neural interfaces to nanotechnology shunts to neutrino-enabled networking prostheses — are strictly regulated by some of the most sophisticated security systems in existence. All wireless communications are blocked from the estate boundary onward, and either Eva or one of her assistants meets all visitors at the door, producing a detailed list of forbidden technology which must be surrendered before entering the house. (Although no scanners are in evidence, the list is invariably comprehensive, detailed, and specific to each visitor.) One presumes that these security systems have been supplied by We, for whom cyber-privacy has always been a central concern, and of whom Eva S has long been a strong and vocal supporter. Indeed, various governments have attempted to requisition the estate's scanning technology in the name of national security, but all such demands have subsequently been quietly withdrawn, likely under direct pressure from We.

afterwards.[9] Once these conditions have been agreed to, visitors are free to browse the archive and listen as they choose.

After visitors have explored the archive, however, Eva S encourages them to share these stories in the spirit of the original reading, preferably in as open and public a venue as possible. (Indeed, the so-called Smutsters have enthusiastically adopted this directive in both their guerrilla performances and more formal readings, which range from the impromptu and improvised to more "authentic" reproductions of the original Mother's Day event.)[10] Ms. S describes

[9] In the case of visitors arriving alone, Eva S or one of her assistants will typically take on this companion role. Indeed, in my own solo visits, Eva and her assistants have not only joined me for as many hours as I have chosen to listen but have also proven incredibly forthcoming in our subsequent explorations. Contrary to what one might expect from her aggressive stances and flamboyant accessorizing as a performer, Eva tends more towards comfort than style in dress. An older woman with greying hair, she often sips herbal tea as she calmly describes her own erotic reaction (or lack thereof) to the recording under discussion, occasionally slipping into reminiscences of the visitor who originally recited it. For anyone seeking to explore these stories, I would highly recommend such a visit.

[10] The designation *Smutster* was originally coined in 2030 as a derogatory term for Eva S's exponentially growing legion of fans. However, the term was reappropriated almost immediately by those same fans and aggressively refined over the decades, such that it now refers more narrowly to aficionados of the Tio Boop stories rather than fans of Eva's work as a whole. The Smusters' "authentic" readings — although their authenticity has never been endorsed by Eva S as such — strive to reproduce the original Erotica and Pornography Night described in the Eighteen Year Letter as faithfully as possible. Traditionally, these events are held at a faux-European café (even in continental Europe, some faux-European cafés have sprung up to cater to purist Smutsters), with a row of espresso machines in the back, lighting systems rigged with slow-timed dimmers to mimic the fading Edmonton light, and as many additional supporting details as the organizers can manage. Each event opens with the alleged epigraph to Tio Boop's original reading and consists of four reading slots, including a last-minute reshuffle of the reading order due to the (also traditional) absence of the first reader. The final reading slot is

the maintenance (and oral dissemination) of this archive as her tribute to Tio Boop, without whose original reading she would quite literally not exist.[11] She further claims that

---

typically held open in case Tio him or herself should show up, and when Tio invariably fails to arrive, the remainder of the reading may proceed in any number of ways. The final reader may be arranged in advance or selected from the audience, either by random ballot or some more spontaneous method, such as a blindfolded organizer picking a person from the crowd by touch alone. Some purists omit the final reading entirely, observing a minute of silence, while others read from bootleg transcripts of "original" stories allegedly heard at the 2009 event. Indeed, debates over the appropriate means of handling these finer details have often led to significant splits within the Smutster community. When participating in these events both as a fan in my teens and later while researching my master's thesis, I always preferred the minute of silence, during which — if only for a moment — I could close my eyes and imagine Tio right there in front of us, about to begin. However, even the most "authentic" of these readings stop short of reproducing — at least on any formal level — the post-reading events described in the Eighteen Year Letter. For an in-depth study of these practices within the broader context of the Smutster movement, see *Smutsters Unite! Sexual Revolution in the 21st Century: A Case Study* (Quinlan, 2045).

11 Due to her status as one of the earliest and most thoroughly documented "We-orphans" of the late '20s and early '30s, no official records exist for Eva S before 2028. She maintains that she was raised by her five parents until the age of eight, when one of Peter Smith's legal challenges gained enough traction to have her removed from the family. However, Smith's concurrent bid for sole custody was unsuccessful, and Eva was placed into foster care until age eighteen, when she received two letters. The first, written as an "insurance policy" in case the worst happened and Peter succeeded in breaking up the family, described the unusual circumstances of Eva's conception. The second letter arrived enclosed with the first, a cryptic missive from the group We, detailing Smith's ongoing harassment of Eva's birth family even after her removal. In response, the family had accepted an offer from We to erase all records of their existence, and now the organization was making that same offer to Eva. Eva immediately accepted, thereby neutralizing Smith's harassment, and asked to be reunited with her family. Shortly after this reunion, Eva began producing her own erotic performance art. Unlike many early We-orphans, Eva was never brought up on charges of fraud or identity theft (possibly because of her sudden fame) and was in

through sharing these stories — and the intensive subjective engagement arising from this in-person sharing — Tio Boop's purpose will inevitably manifest itself, that purpose being not merely to titillate but to free people to share and explore their own erotic fantasies and stories and, more importantly, to learn to *enjoy* these stories without guilt or fear of reprisal.[12]

---

fact a key promoter of We's emergence into the public sphere in the late '20s. (Although it remains difficult to determine with any certainty, anecdotal evidence suggests that We had been operating covertly since at least 2004, and many We-orphans resorted to identity theft as a means of survival.) However, it was not until We's cyber-erasure of several world leaders in 2034 — including the acting President of the United States — that worldwide legislative reform provided legal status to the growing legion of We-orphans. To this day, despite her extraordinary candour regarding the details of her own life, Eva has refused to identify anyone from her pre-We past by either their current or "real" name. Certain scholars have argued that Eva's entire backstory may be fabricated, but the demonstrable existence of We — along with Eva's longstanding and well-documented connections to that group — seems to support Eva's version of events. Moreover, I can personally attest to at least some of We's activities around that time, since in 2028, when I was thirteen, the group abruptly and thoroughly erased both my own and my father's files. To the best of my knowledge, this was the only time We ever erased private citizens' files without their explicit request and permission.

12 Over years of visiting the archive, first while researching my dissertation and later in support of my ongoing scholarly work, I have found it impossible to predict how any given listener will react to a particular story. Furthermore, I can personally attest to the fact that not all — indeed, not even the majority — of the archived stories are titillating in the sense of provoking sexual excitement. Certainly, some do (and powerfully so), but others may be heard from a more distanced, almost anthropological perspective. But however devoid of erotic impact (or even downright repulsive) they may be, a current of vulnerability runs through them, a sense that each story somehow reflects the recorded speaker's entirely uncensored erotic self. And with each new story, the listener may be pulled further into the profoundly *human* character of each telling. Rather than blurring together into a mind-numbing catalogue of increasingly banal and mechanized sexual acts, each story becomes *more* particular, more visceral, more differentiated from every one that came before. Indeed, over the course of several stories, the listener may gain a stronger and stronger

In her own work, in accord with her manifesto, Eva S has
consistently aimed at enlarging the realm of erotic possibility, encouraging her audience (and the world at large) to
move beyond the guilt so deeply and commonly ingrained
in certain ways of looking at sex and sexual desire.[13] Her
most recent work ("Long Time Coming," 2049), for example,
explores the possibility that even the infamous "Peter Smith"
may have been as much a victim as a proponent of the conservative "family values" he so vehemently espoused.[14] In it,
noting the one in three chance that Mr. Smith was indeed her
biological father, she explores how Smith's persistent guilt
over his participation on the night of her conception could
have fuelled his two-decade quest to reclaim the child he

---

sense of having almost been there for the original reading, as if slowly
being convinced, cajoled, and freed to tell her own story in response, and
this anachronistic sense of presence may help to explain how this archive
of "original" stories has proliferated and expanded beyond all mathematical
possibility to contain hundreds (possibly thousands) of stories. And yet,
impossible or not, I have studied these stories and their variations for
several decades now, and I can attest with great confidence — my former
co-editors' objections notwithstanding — that *they are all genuine.*

13 See Eva S's uncharacteristically direct "Manifesto" (2033), another early
performance piece. See also Dulles and Candle's essay in Part 4 of this
volume for an intriguing use of this piece as an interpretive lens through
which to (re)read some of Eva's earliest work ("Manifesting the Manifesto:
Exposures, Recoveries, and Complications of the 'Political' in Eva S's Early
Performances").

14 At various times, Peter claimed to be Eva's rightful guardian, her
estranged uncle, and even her biological father, but since his attempts
to force a DNA test failed, these claims remain unverified. In all his legal
battles with Eva's family, Smith consistently appealed to "family values,"
thereby securing financial and legal support from a variety of conservative
political and religious groups. Nonetheless, when one of these well-funded
custody challenges proved (temporarily) successful in removing Eva from
her family, Peter was disqualified as a suitable guardian on the basis of his
own participation — however disavowed and regretted after the fact —
in the "sordid" circumstances of her conception.

genuinely believed to be his daughter.[15] If, she implies, Peter Smith had been free to construct his erotic self on his own terms — and to partake in the incredible erotic diversity of the world around him — he might not have felt such a compulsion to impose received notions of sexual morality upon his own former sexual partners.

Ultimately, this is why I have upheld the original decision to omit all transcriptions of Tio Boop's original story from this collection. Not, as my former co-editors insisted, because of their unreliability or potential to offend, but out of respect for the story itself. As Ms. (or Mr.) Boop so succinctly put it, this ever-proliferating story is not for reading, but for telling, and to pin it down to any singular or static representation would violate the very deepest principles of Boop's (and by extension Eva's) artistic project. Rather, I strongly encourage readers to visit the archive and hear these stories for themselves. Immerse yourself in them, surrender to their rhythms, their internal logic, and explore what sensations may come. Let them under your

---

15 My father and I were never close. He never approved of my studies and wasn't shy about saying so at every opportunity. Ever since I attended my first Smut Story reading at the age of fifteen, he hated what he called "that goddamn smut stuff" and found it intolerable that any daughter of his would demean herself by becoming involved with it in any way. Six months ago, for the first time, he told me why. He was, he said, the very same "Peter Smith" who had worked so hard to remove Eva from her family, and he sincerely believed he was her father. His voice shook as he apologized for disparaging my studies and told me how deeply he now regretted his nineteen-year persecution of Eva and her family. Then he entrusted me with what he called his own "Forty-nine Year Letter," which he asked me to deliver to Eva, sealed and in person, upon the event of his death. He also had me hold the microphone to his lips as he finally told the story he heard on that fateful night. This, I was to deliver into the Smut Story archive on his behalf, if Eva would accept it. He was very ill, and prone to rambling towards the end, so these could simply be the dementia-fuelled inventions of a dying man. Nonetheless, I have delivered — along with the letter and the tape — my own half of the DNA evidence required to verify at least one part of my father's story. The rest is up to Eva.

skin, where they can expose the contours of your own hidden stories. Then pass them on to friends, lovers, or even strangers — none of these being mutually exclusive categories, of course — along with your own, ultimately mingled and mixed, indistinguishable, the one from the other.[16]

16 Take Peter's story, for instance. It has been added to the archive, and you can ask for it by name. I have listened to it several times now, with Eva. Now it's your turn. Take it, listen, and find out for yourself. There is no knowing how it will strike you. You might turn it into a joke. Or dismiss it. But know that for one person at least, if only for a moment, it was true.

THE EVERETT-WHEELER HYPOTHESIS
(OR, THE MANY-WORLDS INTERPRETATION)

I. RETROVIRUS

El is the first.

When they cross paths at a mutual friend's open mic night, her unruly mass of red curls is the first thing to catch his attention. She's thin and pale, almost waifish. Leaning forward in her seat, she never takes her eyes off the performers or gives even the slightest indication that she hears the boisterous conversations swirling around her. She might as well be alone. Matthew pegs her as shy, bookish, and soft-spoken. Only a habitual reader could sustain that sort of focus. But when a break between performers arrives, she speaks and proves him wrong.

It takes a full half-hour for Matthew to work up the nerve to invite her outside for a smoke, and even then the first few drags pass in awkward silence before he can force himself to say something, anything. But from the moment the word *ethnobotany* passes his lips, he is entirely relieved of that responsibility as El enthusiastically recounts the ongoing trial-and-error appropriation, patenting, and biopiracy of traditional herbal knowledge by western medicine, from willow bark (aspirin) to rosy periwinkle (vinblastine) to cinchona bark (quinine).

"I mean, it's been going on for *literally* centuries! They just go in there, pretending they want to learn from the local shamans and traditional practitioners. And they're all like, 'Please, let us learn this deep and sacred wisdom of your people so we can help ours.' Then they take a shitload of samples, pump the practitioners for information on how it all works, and patent the whole process." El pauses to light another cigarette. "Then they turn around and come out with a 'new' wonder drug, or a cure for whatever-it-is, and sell it as their own 'invention.'" She emphatically air-quotes each suspect term, and Matthew isn't sure whether to nod or shake his head. He goes with the nod. "No credit or compensation to the people who gave them the information, the ones who showed them there was anything there to *investigate* in the first place! Nothing. Not a penny. No acknowledgement. And that's just the start! Did you know they're patenting people's *genes*?" El pokes her cigarette at Matthew for emphasis.

Matthew smokes, nods, and murmurs at what he hopes are appropriate points as she tells him about the drug companies' complicity in land theft, monocropping schemes, and other practices essentially adding up to cultural genocide. And he finds — much to his surprise — that he agrees with almost everything she says. By the end of night, they have established a shared disillusionment with their formal studies (his in physics, hers in biochem), a common fascination with alternative belief systems, and a matching aversion to prematurely committed relationships. The next day, they meet for vegetarian dinner, consume countless cigarettes and pints of draft, close out not one but two increasingly deserted bars, and finish off the evening with a night-capping joint at his place. The sex is transcendent, and within a month they're effectively living together. Matthew's housemates think she's amazing. And he agrees.

The conversation begun that first night continues in bed, over meals, at bars and coffee houses, amidst clouds of smoke (pot and tobacco), acoustic protest music, and old folk standards. They share a fascination with the Hidden World and agree that their respective disciplines have a disturbing tendency to deny their roots in preceding belief systems, the Enlightenment having generated some sort of strange cultural amnesia, a deeply psychotic break in western historical consciousness. El knows too much about the mechanisms, origins, and shortcomings of prescription drugs to accept western medicine as axiomatic, and Matthew knows too much physics to see the world as anything but a series of hidden correspondences, reality occluded by the limited mechanisms of human perception.

For Matthew, the occult is more a way of thinking than a set of specific labels or practices. As both scientists and shamans know — at least the good ones — one culture's magic is another's science. Even the word *occult* simply means *hidden*, and the scientific world is entirely composed of just such occult patterns: atomic numbers and weights, electrons and protons, probability waves and Fourier transforms. Transcendental numbers like pi lie at the heart of even the simplest geometrical shapes, and the "natural" logarithm lurks deep in the roots (and stems and petals) of every biological system. In his compulsive attempts to understand these hidden patterns — including the (repressed, ignored, or unnoticed) connections between them — Matthew reads books upon books upon books, takes electives in anthropology, psychology, and literature, and writes countless term papers on witchcraft and the occult.

Where Matthew constructs intellectual models and arguments, El absorbs the occult directly from the world around her. She attracts a constant stream of aging hippies and potheads, drawn like metal filings to the magnet of her belief and more than happy to read her stars, aura, palm, or tea leaves. An outspoken atheist, El nonetheless accepts the underlying connection between body and spirit as a given, the missing link between traditional practices and modern medicine. For her, tarot and astrology are far more plausible tools for self-examination than some nineteenth-century quack's "talking cure." (Freud was an asshole, a rape apologist — or more accurately, denier — and a patsy of the upper-class fathers who abused their daughters then hired him to cover it up. And Jung wasn't much better.) She takes great joy in noting that reiki, acupuncture, shiatsu, and other traditional therapies have far longer pedigrees — and have therefore been more thoroughly tested over the centuries — than the vast majority of western medical practices. And she accepts them all as they are offered.

Sometimes, while feigning interest in the latest yahoo's ramblings, Matthew finds himself wishing he could share her instinctive, visceral belief in even the most dubious practices and practitioners, so different from his compulsively analytic, abstract model-building. So unfiltered, immediate, and open. He hates thinking of El — so brilliant in other contexts — being taken in by a series of flakes and posers. But more than that, he hates that these same flakes and posers share something with El that he cannot, no matter how hard he tries.

"So did you read it yet?" Matthew asks while chopping zucchini for the stir fry. El tosses the first bowl of ingredients into the wok, and the aroma of frying garlic and onions fills the kitchen. Matthew has already begun to associate that smell with her, and he loves it.

"Finished it yesterday," says El. "Pass me the ginger?"

Matthew passes the shredded ginger and plate of cubed tofu over to El, who adds them to the mixture, along with a splash of soy sauce.

"And?"

For weeks now, Matthew has been trying to get her to read *The Serpent and the Rainbow*, Wade Davis's first-hand account of his investigation into the real-world existence of Haitian zombis. It's where Matthew learned the term ethnobotany in the first place, making it indirectly responsible for their first real conversation, and he's deeply curious to see what she thinks of it. He sets the bowl of chopped zucchini on the counter by El and starts in on the broccoli.

"It was okay, I guess."

"Just okay?"

El looks up from her stirring.

"I mean, he single-handedly figured out the whole zombi thing. How cool is that? And not just the chemical formula either. The whole cultural context."

"Yeah, I guess so," says El. "I mean, I see what you're saying. It's just —"

"Just what? Seriously, he *proved* they're real. Score one for the good guys, right?" Davis was the first outsider to learn the precise methods of preparing the zombi poison, a catatonia-inducing paralytic, and he did it by taking Vodoun practitioners' direct testimony and beliefs seriously, something no one before him had done. "Turns out Vodoun isn't superstition, it's bona fide *science.*"

"Well, yeah, but I mean, he was hired by a pharmaceutical company, right?"

"Sure, they underwrote the whole thing. Wanted new and better anaesthetics."

"And what did he do when he got back?"

"He wrote the book! You know, the one you just read? Documenting how Vodoun generated pharmaceutical insights western scientists hadn't even thought of?"

El picks up the cutting board and dumps the broccoli into the wok as Matthew starts de-stringing the snow peas.

"No, I mean what did he do with the formula? He sold it to the pharmaceutical company that hired him, right?"

"Well yeah," says Matthew, "it's what they hired him for."

"And did he pay his informants? The members of the secret societies?"

"I don't know. I mean, he wrote a book about them. Showed that Voudonists aren't some kind of superstitious 'savages,' that they've got an internally consistent system of cultural knowledge that actually *works*. Isn't that a good thing?"

"And who got the royalties from the book?"

"He didn't make much on the book."

"And the movie?"

"What does the movie have to do with anything?" Matthew doesn't see the point of this line of questioning. Sure, Davis made a shitload on the movie. And the movie truly, deeply sucked. But still. "You read the preface, right? The part where he said the movie was a strategic trade-off to fund future projects *without* selling out to the pharmaceutical companies?"

"Yeah, I know." El tosses the finished snow peas and a can of sliced water chestnuts into the wok, producing a great hiss and burst of steam. She speaks louder to be heard over the sound of frying vegetables. "I get that he was well-intentioned. But I still can't tell if he really understood or respected the source tradition. Presumably they call them secret societies for a reason, right? Would they really want him telling just anyone about that stuff? I mean, he took secret, sacred knowledge and *published* it."

THE EVERETT-WHEELER HYPOTHESIS

"Okay, but would you even know that if Davis hadn't told you so himself? He was *trying* to do the right thing, to give *context.*" Matthew picks up the boiling egg noodles and drains them into the sink. "Shit! Fuck! Ow!"

"Here, give me that," says El, turning on the cold water. "Put your hand under here. It'll help." She tosses the noodles into the wok, another hiss and burst of steam. "I'm just not sure if he really *believed* the practices, you know? He learned them, but only to pull them apart and analyze them. And you lose something when you do that."

"So you thought it was stupid."

"Oh baby, I didn't say that." El takes the wok off the flame and moves it to a hot pad on the table. "Did you forget to eat again? You always get moody and uncoordinated when you haven't eaten."

He hates it when she does that. Sometimes, it's like she can see right through him. He hasn't eaten since breakfast. Matthew turns away to set the table.

Five days into Algonquin Park, they haven't yet encountered a soul, and with practice even the roughest portages have become routine. One pack each, the canoe easily hoisted over their heads, and off they go, back on the water in half an hour at most. The northern route was El's idea, the poorly maintained trails a trade-off for the extra solitude. They are halfway through the portage, and Matthew's in front this time, so he sees the bear first.

The world heaves and shifts, turning subtly perpendicular to itself.

Nothing has changed. The sun still shines through the trees crowding in on either side of the narrow path. The thwart still balances across Matthew's shoulders, its weight mingling with the accumulated heat and discomfort of the portage, the slight bruising of his shoulders, his aching back. The same rocky path stretches out before him, and El still stands right behind him under the canoe, sightline blocked by Matthew's body and probably wondering what's going on.

"Why are we st — ?"

"Ssh!" Matthew hisses and steps to one side, pointing.

No more than twenty feet away, the bear snuffles through a half-filled, half-buried bag just off the portage route. It glances up for a moment, huffs once, then returns to its salvaging. Yet deep in Matthew's gut, the seismic shift persists. Just one more step to cross the event horizon of this moment, over a cliff, and into a falling dream. A deerfly buzzes up under the canoe, circles his head three times, and zips off without landing. Sweat trickles down and drips from his chin to the already soaked front of his shirt.

Matthew takes that step. Then another.

Moving forward again, they walk as lightly and quietly as possible, the sound of their laboured breathing echoing, amplified by its confinement within the canoe's fibreglass hull. The hum of insects and thump of boots on hard-packed earth are maddening distractions, masking any warning of what might await around each blind corner. Even once they've passed beyond sight of the animal, the mere memory of its hulking muscular mass — that head alone easily the length of Matthew's thigh — transforms the benign ambience of the shaded woodland trail, each snapping twig or movement in the underbrush another threat of ambush.

Reaching the water, they wordlessly load their packs and launch the canoe, maintaining that silence until they're well out from shore. El speaks first.

"It was just so weird! Like I wasn't even surprised." She's grinning.

"You mean, you . . ."

"All morning, I *knew* something was coming. I could *feel* it. I didn't know what until I saw it, but then it was like, *Oh right, that*. Calm, you know?"

"Calm, right. Yeah . . . No." Matthew struggles to suppress his annoyance. "I mean, as much as I love that special sensation of shitting myself, maybe you could give me a little heads-up next time you just 'know' something like that?"

El laughs at that, so Matthew edges forward to kiss the nape of her neck before climbing back over the thwart to his seat, steadying the rocking canoe with hands on both gunnels. No point in arguing. Better to relax into the flash of sunlight on water, the meditative splash of paddles, and accept El's joy in her own perception of the event. Even Davis couldn't simply will himself into direct belief. At best, all he could do was observe, analyze, and try to understand his informants' behaviours.

Later, while trying to lob a rock-ballasted rope over a branch high enough to hang the food and reduce the odds of bear encounters, Matthew tries again to share El's enthusiasm for that improbable moment of retroactive clairvoyance. He wants to believe as she does, without hesitation or analysis. But as always, he finds himself looking in from the outside, compulsively translating El's perceptions into a language his mind can accept. On his eighth failed attempt, El asks why he's bothering to hang the food at all.

"I told you there's nothing to worry about, right?"

"Yup."

"I mean, the feeling's totally gone."

Matthew re-ties the ballast rock, and this time the rope sails high and clear over the branch. "Yup, I hear you," he says, securing the rope's free end to a convenient sapling. "No worries at all."

Later, Matthew lies awake for what feels like hours listening to the sound of El's undisturbed, slow breathing. Not until he fetches the tissue-wrapped condom from the tent floor, seals it in a Ziploc, and lowers and re-hoists the packs by flashlight is he finally able to drift off to sleep. Even then, with the cooking clothes, dishes, organic waste, and food suspended high above the forest floor, his dreams are filled with images of that massive head, snuffling, searching, and rooting about for that one lingering, vagrant scent. Razor-sharp claws slashing the flimsy intimacy of their nylon tent, jaws closing, locking, and refusing to release.

When they move into their own place, some things change, and sex is the first thing to go. From headaches to gastric problems, the reasons are so clichéd that at first Matthew tries to turn it into a joke. That doesn't go over so well. Next, he blames himself. Has he been taking her for granted? Perhaps he's been shirking more practical duties, like cooking and cleaning. Typical guy-moves-in-with-girlfriend mistakes. But while El seems to appreciate the sudden spate of clean dishes and elaborate candlelit dinners, she invariably refuses the accompanying wine, and the evening ends as always, terse, strained, and silent.

When El quits smoking, Matthew does his best to be supportive. It isn't hard to smoke outside, and tobacco-free joints are no great hardship. Even when she begins to insist, first, that he brush his teeth before kissing her, then that he wash his hands and face as well, it's an inconvenience but not the end of the world. At first, it's just that the smell bothers her, but then it starts making her nauseous, and what kind of asshole would want his girlfriend to kiss him when it makes her feel sick? Of course, quitting smoking means cutting back on drinking as well, which means she doesn't like to go out so much if it involves alcohol. But this too is understandable, and they compensate by having more potluck dinner parties with friends. And if Matthew occasionally wants to go out for a drink or four with friends, he can still go on his own.

The thing with the bike catches him by surprise, though. After all, without El's encouragement, he never would have had the nerve to buy the aging CB750 in the first place. She had loved the hulking steel beast, the whole outdated nostalgia of it. She had even lied to her mother — a woman whose first evaluation of Matthew had been that he seemed like a nice boy, too bad he was going to die in a horrible crash — swearing up and down that she would never ride such a dangerous machine. In the beginning, they often went for long weekend rides, random back-road adventures punctuated by stops in small towns or impromptu picnics in empty fields. Her arms wrapped tight around his chest, the roar of the engine, and the wind in their faces. More than once she had ordered him to pull over, fairly vibrating with excitement as she dismounted from the bike and tore at his clothes, dragging him off the road to make urgent love barely concealed by the adjacent trees or long grass.

"It's like *flying*," she would say, and Matthew knew that she too was feeling that rush of sudden weightlessness at the top of each rise, each sharp dip in the road, as if together they were escaping gravity itself. And perhaps because of the intimacy of the shared lie — to her mother and to his own parents, who don't even know he has a bike license, let alone a bike — the motorcycle has become (for Matthew) emblematic of their relationship. Even poorly tuned, smelling of gasoline, and with a growing hole in the muffler, it represents their freedom to jettison all external obligations, all expectations, parental and otherwise, the freedom to just *go*.

But now the lie she fabricated for her mother turns real as El more and more often refuses to ride the bike. The smell of gas is nauseating, the engine too loud, the spare helmet ill-fitting and claustrophobic. Fair enough. If El doesn't want to ride it, she doesn't have to. Matthew starts riding alone. El starts referring to the bike as Matthew's *two-wheeled death wish*, insisting that he drive only during the day, and only when she knows exactly how long he'll be gone. Upon his return, she greets him at the door with graphic descriptions of her psychic paralysis and anxiety-induced vomiting while he was gone.

"It's this horrible feeling," she says. "I just *know* something's going to happen. I can *see* it." She's pale and shaky, her forehead clammy with cold sweat where he kisses it. "The whole time you're gone, I keep seeing you with a broken neck or lying on the road somewhere, bleeding. And nobody knows where you are. It *literally* makes me sick."

"Ssshhh . . ." says Matthew, hugging her close. "Ssshhh, it's okay. I'm here."

"You fucking idiot," she says, shoving him off and stepping back. "I know you're fine *now*. It's not *now* that I'm worried about. It's what's *going* to happen, dammit."

Matthew explains that he's a careful driver, and that the risk of accident drops drastically after the first year of driving (now past), so she has nothing to worry about. When that doesn't work, on longer rides, he starts calling home periodically to check in. As her recurring migraines and bouts of nausea worsen, he stops smoking when she's around. When she quits drinking entirely, he stops bringing alcohol home. But when Matthew's occasional nights out drinking with friends start prompting further accounts of El's nausea and vomiting in his absence (the latter always miraculously ceasing upon his return), his sympathy begins to wane.

For a week, El has been subsisting on nothing but clear fluids and toast. And this time, when Matthew says he's going out for drinks, she rises abruptly from the bed, heads straight to the bathroom, and vomits noisily and productively with the door open. Wiping her mouth on her flannel pyjama sleeve, she returns and sits back down on the bed.

"How can you even think about going out? Don't you even care?"

"Of course I . . . I mean . . . I just need a bit of a break, okay?"

"So you're going out to get shitfaced while I stay here and puke my guts out."

"You know it's not . . . Look, you don't have to wait up. I just —"

"So you're planning to be late."

"I'm not *planning* anything. But you need your rest, and —"

"Wait." She holds up one hand while opening the top dresser drawer with the other. "Just wait . . ." She digs through socks and underwear until she finds what she wants. "Here you go." She places the condom in his hand, folds his fingers over the crinkling plastic wrapper, and pats his closed fist. "One for the road. Just in case."

"Jesus! We're just going for a few —"

"I know! I get it." El glares. "But since you're being all *spontaneous* . . ."

Matthew leaves the room, quietly closing the door behind him. From the living room, he hears El starting to cry and decides to leave the apartment as well. As he closes the outside door, El shouts something, but he can't make out the words. For half an hour, he walks in aimless circles through the neighbourhood.

He returns to find the bedroom trashed, bookshelves dumped, and the futon mattress flipped onto the floor, the wooden frame turned on its side. El lies collapsed on the couch, puffy eyed and staring into space. Matthew sits beside her and waits as her eyes slowly regain focus. When she sits up and starts apologizing, resurgent sobs fragment her sentences into a series of disjointed phrases. Matthew lays her back down on the couch, silently rubbing her shoulders as she cries herself to sleep, which takes about five minutes. He calls his friends, cancels his plans, and reconstructs the demolished bedroom. Then he undresses, climbs into the remade bed, and lies sleepless as he turns the situation over and over in his head.

When inexplicable rashes join the migraines, nausea, and vomiting, Matthew is forced to reassess. Tantrums or no, you can't just *invent* a skin condition. Shiatsu, reiki, and acupuncture (all free from friends) help a little, but the underlying symptoms persist. El says she would consult a homeopath if she could, but her health plan doesn't cover it. Doctors are less than useless, prescribing everything from antacids to pregnancy tests, none of which produce even a hint of a solution. No one explicitly suggests the possibility of an eating disorder, though several doctors pointedly comment on El's sudden weight loss. Half of them seem to think she's either hypochondriac or just plain crazy, and El finally admits that sometimes she wonders too.

"I mean, what if it's all in my head?"

She sits on the rickety Sallyanne-salvaged recliner, eyes red from crying, her cheeks, forehead and chest a welter of irregular raised red blotches, balled up tissues lying in drifts on the floor around her. Matthew takes on the role of defence cross-examiner.

"What, that rash isn't real?"

"No, but maybe it's just — "

"Stockholm syndrome? Group hallucinations? Because I see it too, you know."

"But maybe . . ."

"No, wait, I know. It's a secret government experiment. X-files stuff." Matthew whistles the signature tune, and El giggles through her tears. An improvement. She still looks like hell, but at least now she's smiling.

"Now you're just making fun of me."

"They're nothing but pill pushers. You know how these people work. If they can't drug it into submission they think it doesn't exist." Matthew carefully climbs onto the recliner and folds her into his side as she tries to pout theatrically, laughs, then cries some more. In the circle of his arms, she feels hollow-boned and birdlike, as if she might break under the slightest pressure. But he holds on tight all the same, and his skin grows slick with snot and tears as she buries her face in the crook of his neck.

El's body has become its own Hidden World — hidden from both of them now — and Matthew sets to work trying to uncover its secrets. Even cursory research confirms that psychosomatic effects are by definition entirely real, that the mind can physically affect the body. Countless case studies confirm it, from the simplest of placebo effects to the medically documented case of a guy whose cancer went into complete remission for over a year, only to return within a week when he learned — in spite of his doctors' attempts to shield him from the knowledge — that the experimental drug therapy he thought was fuelling his remission had utterly failed in clinical trials several months before. Two weeks later, the poor bastard was dead. The more he reads, the more Matthew becomes convinced that El's psyche must be the occulted underlying cause of her illness. He hypothesizes that it's all rooted in fear. Fear of physical harm (fostered by her mother's dark fatalism), fear of abandonment (legacy of her father's departure years before), and generalized fear of loss (loss of Matthew most of all). Worst of all, she obviously has no conscious awareness of any of this.

Based on this hypothesis, Matthew tries to make it clear that none of her fears will materialize. For a month, he does everything she asks: stops riding the bike, drinking, smoking at home, even going out with friends. But El's symptoms get worse, not better, and eventually he admits defeat. He doesn't want to fulfill her subconscious prophecies of doom, but like El, he has no choice and ultimately no control. When he moves out, Matthew feels like shit about it but reasons that if he removes the stimulus (himself), she will eventually recover.

Except he's wrong.

El's mother finally springs for a consultation with a homeopath who immediately tests for allergies. The wheat-germ test patch swells up like a balloon. Within weeks of cutting all wheat from her diet, El is visibly gaining weight, and the rashes, nausea, and vomiting disappear entirely, along with all the other "psychosomatic" symptoms.

Two months later, they sit in El's new living room, her on the chaise lounge, Matthew on the couch. A month ago, he helped repaint this room, rearranging the furniture to accommodate for the missing recliner and futon, which El has since replaced. New plants populate the window sills, and slanting sunlight illuminates the steam rising from their cups of herbal tea. A plate of gluten-free brownies sits on the coffee table between them. This weekly ritual allows them to play the role of best friends, supporting each other through the aftermath of their own breakup. Eventually, she will tell him the first time she sleeps with someone else, and he will pretend it's no big deal. They have become that kind of friends.

"There's something I never told you."

El leans back in her chair, staring out the window, and Matthew wonders if she's about to explain that she once cheated on him or has found a new lover. It could be a pregnancy scare, but all the random testing from the previous months makes that unlikely.

"What is it?"

El takes a breath and releases it in a long, slow sigh, cupping her steaming mug close to her chest. Still looking out the window, she hunches into herself, feet curled up under her, shoulders forward, elbows pulled in close.

"You know I skipped my dad's funeral."

"Yeah?"

"But you don't know why."

"Guy was an asshole, took off on you and your mom. I wouldn't have gone either."

"True, but that's not it."

A long pause.

"God, this is . . . I mean, my therapist thought I should . . ."

El glances at Matthew as if trying to gauge his reaction. He smiles encouragingly, but she's already looking back out the window.

"I just don't want you to . . ." she begins again, then falls silent.

Matthew lets the silence stretch. He can wait. Setting down his tea, he picks up a brownie, takes a bite, and notices a small drop of yellow marring the fake wood grain of the coffee table. They must have missed it while cleaning up after painting, and now it has dried and hardened, a permanent mark.

"It's just that sometimes . . ." El is still speaking to the open window, her voice turned flat and quiet. "Sex with you . . . Sometimes, it reminded me of my father."

This makes no sense. Why would a therapist want El to discuss her daddy issues with Matthew? El doesn't even believe in that Freud crap.

"I mean, at first the sex was great. More than great. Amazing." Another pause, a breath. "But then later, sometimes. Like after we saw the bear, that night in the tent when you covered my mouth and told me to stay quiet. Certain things you did when we were. Having sex. Triggered memories of him. Doing the same things."

No. She can't be saying . . . Matthew can't breathe.

"And once the memories started, it got harder. For me. To be with you. That way." She continues implacably, that same dead voice. "And eventually, I just couldn't."

Blind with fury, Matthew fixates on the yellow paint spot, unable to look up or away for fear of what he might do. For the first time, he discovers what it feels like to truly want to kill a man. He wants to resurrect the bastard so he can do it himself, with his own hands and feet. Or a baseball bat. Something blunt and heavy. He wants to feel the impact. And still she speaks. No tears. Just words upon words upon words.

"It's not your fault. It happened before, with other people. And I always just walked away. I just. Didn't want to talk about it. Ever." El's voice gets louder, a hint of a tremor. "Because I am *not* some kind of pathetic, helpless victim. I *refuse* to be thought of that way." Then lowers again. "But with you I wanted to try to change that. I just. Couldn't."

Matthew feels like puking, and he wants to cry. Instead, he sits and listens, fists and jaw clenched, his entire body shaking with the effort to stay immobile.

"So I never told anyone. Not until my therapist. And now you."

He wants to smash the crappy Salvation Army coffee table with its fake wood grain and that goddamn accusatory paint spot. He wants to break bones, rend flesh, shout, move, scream. He wants someone to pay for this. In a dissociated portion of his mind that somehow remains apart from all this, a calm voice notes, *Someone already has.*

"I'm sorry I didn't tell you before," El concludes. "Maybe it would have made some sort of difference. I don't know."

She's crying now. But Matthew can't look up from the table.

Not yet. And though she's not accusing him of anything, some-how, on some level, he knows it was his fault. He should have known. Stupid fucking paint spot. Every childhood anecdote she ever recounted shifts, freighted with ominous undertones, potential hidden meanings. Like a retrovirus, this knowledge rewrites the past from the inside out. He wants to take El into his arms, but now he's afraid to touch her. Nothing is differ-ent. But everything, everything has changed.

II. PASCAL'S WAGER

Billie and her son are both head turners, hot-tempered, and high energy with matching mischievous grins. She's half-Italian and half-Ghanaian, and shares custody of her three-year-old boy with his father, who is half-Chinese, half-Irish, thoroughly gorgeous, and — as she often points out — a com-plete asshole. Athletic and apolitical, she is nothing like El. Nor is she shy about sharing her personal litany of assholes.

On their second date, after Billie's son has fallen asleep and been put to bed, *Shrek* predictably fails to captivate the two adults. At first, Matthew worries that the boy might wake up and wander into the living room, but Billie insists he can sleep through anything. Afterwards, post-coital on the couch with the flickering half-light of the muted movie still playing over their bodies, she tells him the story of a day at the beach with her friend Jennie's family. She was eighteen at the time.

It was a picture-perfect family outing, complete with a pic-nic lunch, blankets and towels spread out on the hot sand, a rambunctious game of keep-away in the shallows. And when Jennie's father started wrestling Billie for the Frisbee, she thought nothing of it until he grabbed her from behind, clamped a forearm across her windpipe, and shoved her head underwater while grinding his erection against her ass. Billie presses her back against Matthew and pulls his arm forward to hook it around her throat. The couch smells of sex and popcorn, and Matthew's erection returns.

"Mmmm . . . Yes, just like that."

She squirms, compounding Matthew's discomfort, then twists his arm from her throat, spins to face him, and pushes down on his shoulders with both hands as her knee comes up hard and fast between his legs. She smiles sweetly, her knee poised between his legs and lightly brushing his inner thigh. Then she kisses him, long and deep, before sighing and falling aside onto her back.

"Just like that. Except with him I followed through. And you know the best part?"

Matthew shakes his head.

"The very *best* part was watching the bastard try to pretend nothing had happened. Limping up onto the beach, all pale and shaking. He could hardly walk, and he looked so *old*. I think he said he'd twisted his ankle."

"So you're saying you're tough."

"Believe it. This ride's by invitation only. Speaking of which . . ."

She kisses him again.

Later, Matthew wishes he could be more surprised by the story itself. Appalled, yes — and disturbed by his own arousal at the time — but not shocked. And he hates the empathy that implies. Hates that he could on any level, however subconscious, understand a man who took the mere fact of a woman's beauty as an invitation. But Billie doesn't worry about such abstractions. Nothing seems to get to her.

Another time, while going down on him, she pauses to point out the three crooked fingers on her left hand, souvenirs from the time her ex-husband slammed her hand in the bedroom door for some reason she can no longer recall, breaking each finger between the second and third knuckle. And though

Matthew is starting to get used to these random interjections, this one comes close to derailing him entirely. Nonetheless, she picks up where she left off, expertly bringing Matthew to climax. As if for her, these stories are less a turn-on (or off) than a non-event. A random, recurring aside.

Matthew marvels that these experiences haven't made her uncomfortable with sex, or men, or him. But the more accustomed he becomes to these stories in practice — even beginning to half-expect their arrival at moments of (his own) heightened arousal — the more uncomfortable they make him in principle. As if his head is being carefully, progressively cross-wired. How fucked up would it be to develop some kind of weird Pavlovian response to stories of sexual violence? And yet, her utter lack of fear combined with that matter-of-fact openness is also an incredible relief. Unlike El, Billie puts everything right up front. No secrets, no hangups. What you see is what you get. And god she's hot.

Billie and El do have one thing in common, though. Like El, Billie is fascinated with the occult. But where El actively explored it through communities of belief, Billie says she has no choice in the matter. The occult has always forced itself upon her, manifesting in strange, uncontrollable powers she can neither discount as imaginary nor explain away, and she has learned to deal with these intrusions as best she can.

She says she remembers flying — not jumping or falling, but flying — from a raised porch to the ground below. She must have been eight or nine, awakening with the sun on a fresh spring morning. Knowing better than to wake her parents, she crept out the front door and onto the porch, the weathered planks cool on the soles of her bare feet. She surveyed the empty street, alone in a pristine, prelapsarian world, the soft breeze ruffling her pyjamas. Looking down, she saw her Tonka truck and plastic shovel sitting abandoned on the dry, bare earth, just beyond a ten foot wide strip of fresh sod.

The day before, she had "helped" her father lay that sod, scooping dirt into the toy truck and moving it from place to place. Now she wanted to surprise him by getting started before he was even awake. He would be so proud. But she didn't want to tramp barefoot through the cold, wet dew. She didn't think about it, simply closed her eyes, lifted one bare foot into the air, stepped forward into space, and floated down like a bit of dandelion fluff to land lightly on dry earth. When Matthew asks if she might have imagined it, she says absolutely not. She vividly remembers that sense of relief at having solved the problem, her warm, dry feet planted firmly on the cool earth next to the truck and shovel.

Most of Billie's childhood abilities — flying, preternatural hearing, sensing people's thoughts, occasional invisibility — vanished with the onset of adulthood. Now they manifest in smaller ways: premonitory dreams, occasional flashes of insight, random urges and certainties upon which she invariably acts. Like the time she knew that her son simply *must not go* with his father. She swapped weekends at the last minute, inventing a scheduling conflict, and was later entirely unsurprised to learn that her ex's Tercel had been broadsided by an suv running a red. The impact had crumpled the passenger door, and the police, upon noticing the demolished car-seat, said it was lucky that seat was empty. But Billie knows it wasn't luck.

Matthew doesn't exactly believe these stories. But since El, he has resolved to withhold judgement. At least provisionally. He has learned his lesson. He will enter Billie's Hidden World as far as she will let him. No longer looking in from the outside, he will respect this gift for what it is. A rare and precious point of entry.

And yet, Billie doesn't romanticize her abilities. She can't afford to. Not since her ex pulled that bullshit custody suit. So now she keeps her personal information — anything even remotely medical, sexual, or psychological — off the grid as much as possible. No paper records, walk-in clinics only, cash transactions. False names if absolutely necessary. Even her involvement with Matthew must be kept secret. It's not so much that she doesn't trust people as that she doesn't trust the system and what it would make of her if given the opportunity. After all, they almost had her committed and Aaron taken away based on her ex's testimony. It would have worked, too, if she hadn't hired an investigator to systematically blow his credibility all to hell. What with the gambling, drugs, and so on, the bastard is lucky he gets to see his son at all. Still, she has to be careful. Because while committal and institutionalization themselves don't scare her — she's tough, after all — there is nothing she would not do for her son. Nothing.

Eventually, she trusts Matthew enough to tell him about the one thing she does fear, what she calls — with clearly audible capitalization — the Presence. It whispers from the depths of her subconscious, tugging strings, dropping hints. It is the source of all her abilities, and it wants *her*. She can feel its hunger. Given half a chance it would dance her body like a marionette, and if it ever got out, she would be held at the mercy of something utterly alien, infinitely stronger than her, stronger even than her love for her son. At moments like these she sometimes considers committing herself, except then there would be no one to protect Aaron from her ex. So she holds on, fighting to maintain control in any way she can.

Matthew tries to calm her fears by explaining that the Hidden World *isn't* human — not in the usual sense — which is why such encounters can often be disorienting, even upsetting. But they can also tear away the veil, if only for a moment, providing deeply transformative moments of direct insight.

If it were him, he would risk almost anything for that sort of insight.

"Have you thought about letting it out to see what it wants?" he asks.

They sit on Billie's front porch, perched on the sun-faded outdoor couch as she talks and bums occasional drags from Matthew's cigarette. She's been trying to quit, using everything from the patch to lozenges to inhalers, but nothing seems to stick. Lately, she's been chewing nicotine gum, but certain conversations require a proper smoke.

"What if it takes over and I can't put it back?"

"It doesn't work like that. Think of it this way. You have an incredible gift, this amazing opportunity. This Presence, it's a part of you, not apart from you."

Billie's hands are shaking. He reaches out to put a hand on her arm.

"Don't touch me!" she yelps, flinching away.

As Matthew slowly withdraws his hand, she snags the cigarette from between his fingers — careful not to touch him — and takes a long, slow drag.

"You just don't get it. You don't know it like I do. It's here now. Right *now*. It's just under the surface and it's just . . . waiting. And you. You're so naïve."

"I'm not —"

"Yes you *are*. Don't you see? You're the perfect receptacle. I can feel it feeling you. So eager." Another quick, compulsive drag. "It would swallow you whole."

Matthew lets it go, and Billie pursues her usual strategies, shutting off every avenue the Presence might use to enter her life. Purification rituals excise the past and clear the future: crystals, gestures, and formulae, some adopted from books, others invented. Moving into a new apartment, she lights a smouldering braid of sweetgrass and wafts the smoke into the corners of each room. The sweet-burnt smell lingers for weeks, mingling with that of fresh paint and cleaning products.

The end of her marriage, she says, required a blood ritual to cut and cauterize the connection. She shows Matthew the neat row of four horizontal scars — one for her ex, one for her, one for the relationship, and the last and deepest for her son.

"It went in so smoothly," she says, "like cutting air. And the physical pain... It was like nothing at all. The body... It's like an echo, sometimes, you know? The pain was like that. Nothing more than an echo."

But when she called her ex to describe the process, the razor blade slicing repeatedly through the flesh of her upper arm, he didn't understand the deeper metaphysical nuances. Instead, he assumed she was trying to kill herself and called the cops. She heard the approaching sirens in time to bind the wounds with gauze and throw on a long-sleeved blouse before they arrived. Answering the door, she rolled the cuffs up to her elbows, exposing smooth, unmarked wrists and forearms for their inspection. The officers seemed more bored than anything as she explained that she and her ex were in a custody battle and yes, he was a bit unstable sometimes, but no, she didn't see any need for a restraining order. Her main worry at the time had been that the makeshift bandages might leak, blood dripping down her arm to reveal the location of those wounds, proving her ex's claims that *she* was unstable and giving them an excuse to separate her from her child. And though she has forgiven her ex many things — even allowing him time with their son — she will never, ever forgive him for that.

Two days after their breakup, Billie comes by to drop off a few things.

Predictably, they seduce each other. A bad idea perhaps, but Matthew can't bring himself to feel even the slightest hint of remorse. It's always been this way with her — powerful, impulsive, and entirely irresistible. Lying sprawled amidst the scattered sheets, still sweaty and awash in endorphins, he watches her pick up the Swiss army knife from the bedside table. Naked, cross-legged, and facing him, she opens the blade, tests it against her finger, and draws it lightly across her wrist, following the light tracery of veins up and down her forearm. She sets down the knife to guide his hand across the curve of her stomach, up and over a breast, down again to trace her hip. Her smile hangs suspended somewhere between erotic and resigned as she sets his hand firmly back down on the mattress.

"It's time for me to go," she says.

"Stay. Just for a little while."

"I can't." Again that smile. "It's time."

Billie glances at the clock, then back to Matthew. He tugs her arm, but she remains upright. She said earlier that she couldn't stay long, and he knows this is the day her ex drops off Aaron. Still, he wishes she could put it off just this once. This probably isn't going to happen again, and they haven't even had a chance to talk.

"Just call and say you'll be a little late. Seriously, when was the last time he actually showed up on time for anything?"

"No, it's time, and I want it to be here, with you."

Billie removes his hand from her arm, picks up the knife, and presses the still-open blade lightly against the flesh of her stomach — not enough pressure to cut. Not quite. The blade traces intricate patterns across her abdomen, and she maintains eye contact as the sharp edge clicks softly against her navel ring, once on the way across, again on the return.

He replays the last few minutes' conversation in his mind, and the words click into place: *Here. With you.* Identical words, wrong interpretation. Shit.

Matthew sits up and takes the wrist of her knife-holding hand in his own, feeling her muscles tense as she plants the blade's tip more firmly. And even as he tugs on her wrist — visions of that blade jerking hungrily forward, penetrating flesh with all the eagerness of a former lover granted a moment's return — even in that moment, he can't help wondering. She can't be serious. He pulls harder, wishing for a better grip, but she resists with enough force that he's afraid to let go, even for a moment.

"This isn't funny," he says.

"It isn't meant to be," she agrees.

Billie speaks in the same deadpan tone she used to describe her ex-husband's breaking of her fingers, and Matthew notes those same fingers now jutting awkwardly out from the knife, ring and pinky unable to bend. The Presence is getting stronger, she says, and she's not sure how much longer she can hold on. At least this way, it's her choice. This way, she can still protect her son, if not in the way she had planned. Matthew will take care of Aaron, will make sure he doesn't blame himself and explain that she did this because she loved him.

Matthew has a sudden, vivid image of the blade he never saw, slicing her upper arm so smoothly. (Cutting him off. Bleeding him out.) And for the first time, he considers how Billie's ex must have felt when he got that call.

But if this is a bluff, Matthew doesn't have the nerve to call it. This is Pascal's wager on speed; the stakes are too high. He throws his weight across her body, jerking the knife-hand aside and pinning it to the mattress, holding her down and straddling her hips as she thrashes against him (another echo, this, more recent and inverted). Stripping her of the knife, he sits ungracefully on her stomach, using both hands to fold the blade back into the handle. The moment the blade disappears, she falls still. Then she tells him in that same matter-of-fact tone that this has nothing to do with their breakup. It's just something she has to do.

Matthew releases her, and Billie gathers her clothes and dresses while Matthew leaves the bedroom. In the living room, he hides the knife in his desk. Then he hears a movement behind him and turns to find her standing in the doorway, feet planted wide, a serrated steak knife clenched tight in one raised fist. This time he's less gentle.

He lunges and swats the knife from her hand, drags her back into the bedroom, and pushes her roughly onto the bed. She scrambles to the far corner and curls against the wall, coiled as if ready to spring. Then visibly relaxes. That sad smile is gone, but an underlying wistfulness remains. She sounds almost confused.

"I thought you would . . . understand."

"What, you thought I would just let you — ?"

"It doesn't matter. You're right. I should have known."

"You don't need to do this."

"Yes. I do," she says. Then she stands, pushes past him, and walks out the apartment door into grey drizzle, barefoot in jeans and a T-shirt. Matthew pauses to pull on a robe and shoes and doesn't catch up with her until halfway across the construction site next door.

She doesn't turn, although she must hear his splashing, slip-sliding approach through the ankle-deep mud. Just keeps her head down and marches barefoot through the muck, heedless of the nails and construction debris no doubt lying hidden just beneath the surface. He catches her in a bear hug from behind, pinning her arms at her sides, and though she struggles and kicks, Matthew is just tall enough to keep her feet off the ground the whole way back. As he closes the door and locks the deadbolt, Matthew wonders what the neighbours must think. If it was him, he'd probably call the cops on the crazy guy in the bathrobe.

He shoves Billie into a chair at the kitchen table and plants himself between her and the door. She just sits there, glaring. He can't keep her here indefinitely. But what other option does he have? None at all, he realizes, then finds himself picking up the phone and dialling. It rings twice before picking up, and he doesn't wait for a voice on the other end.

"I need to talk to someone about — "

Matthew stops, realizing he has no idea where to start. Then he sees that it doesn't matter, since Billie sits leaning forward, her finger pressed down on the cut-off switch. Her glare is harder now. Colder.

"What do you think you're doing?"

"I'm calling the fucking *police* is what I'm —"

"You asshole." Billie rips the phone cord from the wall and holds it up in one shaking hand. "You. Fucking. Asshole." She stands and advances. "You really don't get it, do you?"

No, he doesn't. And he's pretty sure he doesn't want to. Matthew remains standing, muscles tensed, ready for anything except what she says next.

"You selfish, self-centered *bastard*. They have *records*. They could *take my son away.*"

Matthew stays utterly still and silent. There's no mistaking the fury in her eyes and stance. This has always been her bottom line, regardless of any contradictions. This is her *son*. Matthew knows that look, and it's got nothing to do with suicide.

"Did you even *think* about the consequences? No, of course you didn't. You don't have a child, don't have the slightest idea what that means. God, you're such an idiot."

Matthew opens his mouth to speak. Then stops. She isn't going to kill herself. Not now. So he resists the urge to argue, to point out the inconsistencies in her logic. He lets her go on, berating his lack of empathy for what it's like to be a single parent. His utter inability to take responsibility for his actions. As her momentum builds and she starts shouting, pacing back and forth around the room, a wave of relief rises, mixing with residual adrenaline to make Matthew's voice shake as he starts to apologize. Of course he wasn't thinking. Yes of course she's right. He wasn't thinking of her son, wasn't thinking at all when he made that call. All he wanted was a way out, someone else to take charge so he could wash his hands of the whole thing.

He barely hears her stream of accusations, his own responses. Anything to keep her focused on that anger, on her son. And it's working. Matthew has no idea what she was thinking before, though his mind keeps spinning, churning up possibilities. (A last-ditch attempt to force his affection? A cry for help? Some sort of blackmail? A bluff? A genuine attempt?) But none of that matters now. All that matters is keeping her focused on her anger at him, the threat to her son. Because whatever it was (a ritual? some kind of sick joke?), it's over now. Now she's talking about the future. Her own future. With both her and her son in it.

"Well I've got news for you, asshole," she says, shoving Matthew aside to retrieve her shoes and start putting them on. "You are not the centre of my universe. The moment you picked up that phone, you blew it. You clearly don't give a shit about me or my son." Billie grabs her jacket from the hook by the door. "Now get out of my way. Aaron's getting home anytime now, and I need to get him back from the other asshole. And don't even think about telling anyone about this. Because if you do, I will fucking end you."

And this time when she storms out of his apartment, the angry slam of flimsy plywood followed by the belated tinny crash of the screen door, Matthew lets her go.

When he calls the next day, Billie acts as if it never happened. Yes, things are fine, and it's no problem if he drops by. She's sure Aaron would love to see him. He checks back every few days that first week, and though Billie's a bit distant and distracted, the boy seems okay. Things return more or less to normal. After a few months — though Matthew still doesn't understand exactly what happened — it becomes clear the crisis has passed. Eventually, Matthew and Billie start sleeping together again, occasionally, impulsively, and recklessly. But never again with any expectations of more. Six months later, apropos of nothing, Billie broaches the topic while waiting in line at the local Tim Hortons.

"It really had nothing to do with the breakup, you know," she says.

"Yeah, you said that."

"I mean, I'm pretty sure it was the Champix."

"The Champix."

"Yeah, well, I was trying to quit smoking, right?"

She says it took a while to figure it out herself. Champix is supposed to interfere with the brain-chemistry of tobacco addiction. Her doctor never mentioned any side effects beyond nausea and occasional headaches, so she didn't put two and two together until she stumbled across the Health Canada advisory online, including the part about psychotic episodes and suicidal ideation. Not common, but enough to be statistically significant.

"So yeah," she finishes. "I just . . . I guess I thought you should know."

III. APOPHENIA

After Billie, Matthew's world devolves into a series of episodic fragments, strange, half-apprehended patterns emerging from the white noise of his life. The closer he looks, the more possibilities he uncovers. And the more explanations he formulates, the more each one contradicts everything that came before. He keeps trying to read his lovers like books, compulsively seeking out the gaps and elisions in each first-person narrative, but each one remains inscrutable, an unsolvable mystery.

On a first date, Matthew raises his hand to brush a stray hair from his eyes, and his date visibly flinches. He asks why, and she says she has no idea where that reaction came from. Perhaps this is true.

Another time, a woman picks him up in a crowded bar — just walks up, sits down beside him, and starts talking. She is very attractive, and they are both very drunk. She invites him back to her place and almost falls over along the way, but Matthew is still just sober enough to catch her and set her back on her feet. Three blocks from the bar, she leads him up a narrow set of stairs to a small, messy bachelor apartment, piles of dirty clothes and unwashed dishes strewn everywhere. She flops bonelessly onto the futon as Matthew closes the door, scoops up a battered guitar from one of the laundry piles, and gingerly negotiates his way to a torn beanbag chair in the far corner. He strums a few chords before settling into fingerpicking exercises, a soft accompaniment to her slurred, rambling monologue. She says she's been cheating on her fiancé for months. Matthew is far from the first, and he won't be the last.

"I guess that makes me a terrible person."
"You don't seem so terrible to me."

"Well, that's where you're wrong," she says, patting the bed beside her. "Anyway, I figure you've got about two minutes before that mellow shit knocks me right the fuck out. So are you going to get over here or what?"

Matthew crosses the room and lies down beside her, fully clothed.

"Just don't come inside me, okay?"

Matthew agrees, and she kisses him. She tastes of cigarettes, strawberry lip gloss, and stale beer. As she clumsily unbuttons his shirt, she keeps repeating slurred variations on that same phrase. "I don't want you to . . ." More kisses. ". . . just don't . . ." The compulsive repetition reminds Matthew of a mantra, or a charm.

She tries to remove his shirt, but it catches at the wrists, and Matthew has to unbutton the cuffs for her. He watches her struggle out of her own shirt, her coordination waning as she sloppily kisses his ear, neck, chest, and stomach. Matthew closes his eyes and succumbs to the sensation of hands and lips on skin, and by the time she reaches his belt, the mantra has faded first to a whisper, then silence. When the silence turns to soft snores, he opens his eyes to find her cheek resting on his stomach, fingers still caught in his belt loop. For a moment, Matthew savours the warm breath on his belly. Then he disentangles himself and returns to the beanbag chair, where he watches her chest rise and fall.

Eventually he stands, slides a pillow under her head, and draws the covers over her sleeping form. He sets the spring-lock to latch behind him, double checks it on his way out, and on the half-hour walk home, he wonders. Something about the whole interaction — something he can't quite put his finger on — makes Matthew feel like that mantra was intended for someone else entirely, not for him at all.

Matthew gives Monique his number at a house party and the next day receives a call from a blocked, private number asking to meet. From that point forward they meet at odd times and locations on a moment's notice: a public park in the middle of the night, the library just after opening, a series of greasy spoon dives during off-peak hours. Matthew keeps forgetting to ask for her number, but since she calls daily it never becomes a priority.

Monique insists upon both instant monogamy and complete secrecy, and Matthew happily complies. She pulls him aside into every empty cloakroom, elevator, or alcove, where they make out like teenagers. At her urging, Matthew tells her his deepest sexual fantasies, along with all the most intimate details of past relationships, confidences she invariably silences with a kiss or strategically wandering hands before he finishes. But no matter how heated things get, she always goes home alone.

When she finally comes over for a nightcap, they barely make it inside before they're tearing at each other's clothes, the wooden door rattling under the force of their long-delayed consummation. Afterwards, she dresses quickly, checks herself in the bathroom mirror, promises to call, and leaves. Matthew stands naked and alone in his empty hallway. It's almost as if she was never there.

The next day, she calls to explain why this has to stop. When she was fifteen she had a thing with a much older man who looked exactly like Matthew. It was intense and sudden, and it ended badly. She gives no further details, and Matthew doesn't ask. She says she hopes they can still be friends.

A month later, Matthew glimpses Monique at a local show and wanders over to say hi at the intermission. She's with a guy named Steve, who immediately launches into the story of how he and Monique met in a Modern American Lit class two years ago. Theirs was a sudden, crazy, whirlwind romance, but somehow the whirlwind lasted. Steve says moving in with Monique two months ago was probably the scariest, best choice he ever made.

Monique calls the next day to thank Matthew for not saying anything. She calls him a sweet, innocent boy, and implores him never to lose that. But this time she says nothing about staying friends.

◦ ◦ ◦

Coincidences multiply like fruit flies and rise in clouds.

A former roommate knows a guy who knows a guy, and Matthew lands a tech-writing job at a television graphic software company. It's not in his field, but the pay's good enough. The office stands at the foot of Billie's street.

On Matthew's third day, Anton shows him the hacked archive of Stephen-in-sales-support's internet porn collection. Anton says he likes messing with the guy, who's clearly an idiot, thinks he's avoided detection just by angling his monitor away from the doorway. Seriously. Meanwhile, Anton's set up an office pool betting on Stephen's next kink-of-the-week. It's hilarious. When Matthew asks about the camera, Anton proudly demonstrates how he's hooked it up to the computer as a live video feed from the street. Not only is it handy for testing the video-capture software, it also doubles as a second window, enhancing the illusion of space in the otherwise cramped cubicle. Observing the image on the monitor, Matthew agrees that it's an ingenious and effective arrangement. And of course it's entirely coincidental that the couch on Billie's front porch falls at the precise centre of the projected image.

Matthew is captivated by Anton's tales of ongoing office hacker-games. Stephen's porn-archive is nothing, a diversion. Even supposedly secure servers — governments, hospitals, banks, credit-card and insurance companies — are relatively easy to crack. The real challenge, says Anton, is gaming companies. Those are the real prize-winners in the monthly competitions. Still, personal data-mining can be fun for the more voyeuristically inclined, and Anton's pet project involves hunting down all his own personal files with an eye towards their potential destruction. Everything is archived, gathered in occult networks of personal information, entire Hidden Worlds at the fingertips of anyone with the skills to access them. For the first time, Matthew begins to understand Billie's wariness over all forms of official record-keeping, her lack of trust in even the supposed anonymity of free STD clinics. He tries to anonymize his electronic presence, to withdraw as much as possible from online networks, but he knows he doesn't have the expertise to do a proper job of it.

As a technical writer, Matthew's job is to interpret, trace, and explain the conceptual black boxes otherwise known as software for an outside audience. But increasingly he can't shut off that habit of compulsive pattern-making. Everywhere he looks, Hidden Worlds multiply and expand, fractally and exponentially. Like crystals materializing from a supersaturated solution, they were always (already) there. Paths of information-sharing. Media consolidation. Conspiracy theories. Information theory. Quantum and number theory. Software design. Half-caught, knowing glances between acquaintances and strangers alike. Random snippets of overheard conversation. Everything is connected. Everything.

Code-worlds, magical systems, theoretical physics, and everyday conversations all blur and run together. He feels constantly surrounded by thronging Presences, all hovering just beneath the surface, ready to rupture the fragile skin of the world at any time. Like El and Billie before him, Matthew confronts the possibility that he may be losing his mind. But it doesn't feel like he's imagining this.

Inexplicably, life continues.

IV. THE GARDEN OF FORKING PATHS

They've never spoken, but he recognizes her from work. The electric blue hair, septum ring and patchwork velour dress are hard to miss. Short and heavy, with an angular face dominated by a too-large-to-be-delicate mole on her left cheek, she's anything but stereotypically attractive. *Striking* is the first word that comes to mind. Yet the extra weight doesn't give an impression of *fat*, exactly. It's more as if something inside her is too vast for containment, too radiant to be suppressed, the sidewalk's ambient gravity field shifting unconsciously to accommodate her passage through the milling lunchtime crowd. She is *expansive*.

She catches Matthew looking and beelines over to halt directly in front of him, well inside his personal space.

"Hi!" she says, and Matthew is struck by how natural it feels to be looking down at that broad grin from mere inches away. "Isn't it a beautiful day?" She touches his arm lightly, and her sweeping look takes in everything — the bustling sidewalk, clear spring sun, and blossoming cherry trees whose shed petals carpet the pavement, crushed underfoot by the constant flow of pedestrians — before returning to him. "I need a hug!" she says, then wraps her arms around him, presses the full length of her body against his, and nuzzles his chest like a cat.

Matthew tentatively, awkwardly returns the hug.

"Thank you! That's just what I needed!" She steps back and extends a hand in more conventional greeting. "I'm Freya. Nice to finally meet you."

Matthew barely has time to shake her hand and mumble his own name in return before she takes his arm, wheels him about, and propels him along the sidewalk. Her words wash over him like a wave-function, patterned yet spreading out into indeterminate clouds of potential. And though he tries to discern some coherence, by the time they arrive back at the office, Freya remains a black box.

As they enter the building, the airy, open-concept design makes discretion impossible, and Matthew wonders how accompanying Freya will affect his social standing in the company. Working in Docs, Matthew occupies the second-lowest rung on the intellectual ladder. (Marketing is lowest but also includes the most attractive men and women in the company, an entirely different category.) Freya, however, is a Developer. And if the company is an empire, the Dev department is a separate, hidden country deep within its heart, the seat of power and culture to which all others defer.

Freya initiates an instant cross-departmental friendship, and over the following weeks Matthew reciprocates as best he can. Luckily, he is entirely accustomed to faking comprehension. Since Matthew documents an API that outside clients can use to customize and control the software, he has to learn how the software works from the inside, from developers. As an outsider barely able to understand (let alone speak) the native language, Matthew sees himself as an ethnological participant-observer, making frequent forays into Dev-land to gather key directions and knowledge from native informants. He then — usually after several dead ends and false starts — collects what little he knows and attempts to translate the arcane, elliptical meanderings of Dev-speak into something at least partially comprehensible, writing and documenting sample API code for customers who are, like him, self-trained amateur programmers.

Developers, by contrast, are the high priests and priestesses of Dev-land, a half-hidden theocracy whose hierarchies have little to do with the company's official management structure. More than mere inhabitants of this land, they are its architects, creating the arcane protocols, structures, and byways of each software package, the very foundations of its Hidden World. In Dev-land, Freya holds (at least) the rank of a minor priestess. Having never documented her group's software, Matthew has no direct connection to her particular sub-cult and therefore only the vaguest idea what she works on. Something to do with graphics, but that could just as easily describe any one of the company's dozen specialized software packages. Nonetheless, her friendship provides a small window into the Dev department's inner workings. Dropping by Freya's cubicle, Matthew learns to laugh at obscure math jokes and memorize the seemingly random strings of numbers and letters used to describe the various Dev-land machines.

In Dev-land, Matthew discovers, computers are the only *machines* (lesser technologies being too unsophisticated to merit such a title) and a knowledge of their relative power provides a key index to any Developer's position within the hierarchy. The better the machine — and the more incomprehensible the software under development — the higher the Developer's rank. One of the true high priests of Dev-land actually writes all of his code in machine language. This isn't a euphemism. Most developers write in high-level, object-oriented languages like C++, with a compiler translating between them and the hardware their software controls and runs on (motherboards, processors, hard drives, and so on). But this man's code requires no translator at all; it speaks directly to the hardware in its own language. And the rumour is, if this particular developer ever left, the hardware interface underlying all of the company's products would have to be redesigned, since no one else can follow the intricate, undocumented products of this one man's (assumed to be brilliant) mind.

This more than anything is how Matthew knows he will never achieve the status of a true Dev-lander. He can write as much object-oriented C++ sample code as he likes, but he simply does not see (or hear, or reason) as a Developer would. However, some of the younger developers share a separate camaraderie, with a slightly differing set of vocabulary and catch-phrases, hints of an entirely different Hidden World. Telltale, glancing references to John Dee, Aleister Crowley, play dates, and Thoth decks. These, he recognizes.

When Freya invites him over, Matthew jumps at the chance. Arm in arm, as has become their custom, they turn onto a tree-lined residential street, where the sprawling four-storey building dominates the block, a nineteenth-century edifice of the sort so commonly turned into rental properties in this part of town. She relinquishes his arm for a moment to point out the anomalous turret (now her bedroom) that once contained the original owner's private library. Sadly, says Freya, the library is long gone, auctioned off with the rest of the house's former contents to endow the will's rent-control and tenant-screening clause. Now a group of Developers and Q/A testers share the space with a random, rotating collection of musicians and artists, the former supplementing the rent of the latter.

Freya leads him up the steps to a heavy oaken door, and Matthew hesitates for a moment, sensing that he is about to cross a profound threshold in ways that have nothing to do with his job. They enter and climb a flight of steep wooden stairs to the first floor landing, where Matthew catches a brief whiff of pot. Through an open door, he glimpses a spacious common area filled with a mismatched assortment of chairs, easels, couches, art supplies, and projects in progress. Open paint cans and half-finished paper maché sculptures, an unidentifiable wire frame, a few covered canvasses. Daren, a Q/A tester from work, sits on one of the couches, holding a lighter to the bowl of a blown-glass pipe. He glances up, and Matthew has a momentary impression of being weighed, measured, and evaluated.

Freya waves to Daren and continues climbing past the open door, tossing words back over her shoulder. "Don't mind Daren. He's not the jealous type, just curious. Gets along great with my boyfriend, and they're not even lovers. Yet."

Though he can't see her face, Matthew hears the implied wink and wonders where he might fit into this particular equation. But the probability wave it describes will no doubt collapse soon enough, and he resolves not to make assumptions. Another flight of stairs, and they pass a second large common area, this one unoccupied.

When Freya pauses on the sun-drenched landing between the third and fourth floors, Matthew takes the chance to catch his breath. A large black cat lies basking on the window sill. Freya scoops it up, holds it to her face, and nuzzles. The cat purrs impressively as she holds it out to Matthew for a proper introduction.

"This is Legba," she says.

As Matthew scratches behind Legba's ears, the purring amplifies and the cat presses his head into Matthew's hand, craning his neck back to expose a soft, vibrating throat. Freya smiles, and Matthew asks the obvious question.

"Is he named for all of them, or just one in particular?"

Freya tilts her head and looks Matthew up and down.

"Not many people would know to ask," she says.

As if he just confirmed something. A moment of recognition.

Like the complexities of Dev-speak, such co-recognitions depend upon an intricate network of social cues, vocabulary, and phrases. And since Matthew first heard of this place, this eclectic commune of bohemians, developers, musicians, and artists, he's suspected it may double as a haven for occult practice, possibly a coven. What with the casual drug use, hints of polyamory, and sheer variety of magical practitioners and systems in conversational evidence both here and at work — from Crowley to Dee to straight-up Vodoun — he would guess chaos magic, but it's hard to say for sure.

As for his conversational gambit — the Legba thing — he won't realize his error until much later. In his attempt to show off his (mostly second-hand) knowledge, he has confused "Legba" with "loa." Legba, lord of the crossroads and the first-invoked spirit in any Vodoun ceremony, is only one of many loa, a generic term for the most powerful of *Les Invisibles*, the spirits who collectively inform and direct every aspect of the material world. But Legba also manifests in several aspects and may therefore be referred to by some initiates as plural. This lucky coincidence covers Matthew's gaffe and may even add to his not-quite-accidental façade of insider knowledge.

But for now, following Freya up the narrow stairs to her room, Matthew remains entirely unaware of his mistake. And he dares to hope that this time, he may finally be able to enter this cabal within a cabal, this second-degree Hidden World.

When Matthew and Freya become lovers, he discovers he was right about Daren, who is another of her many lovers. Now, when Freya stops by his desk, Matthew catches himself glancing around the office, wondering who besides the three of them might know about this arrangement and what those hypothetical others might think of it if they do. But even as his work sags under the twin weights of insomnia and obsession — late nights with Freya and her housemates only compounding his compulsive pattern-making — Matthew's Dev-land excursions become remarkably efficient. Thanks to Freya, he now shares a common language with at least some of the inhabitants, a makeshift pidgin of Docs and Dev with a smattering of occult references. Some of the younger developers even start (covertly) accepting his input on interface design.

He has become hybrid, neither Docs nor Dev, yet partaking in both.

If anything, the low-level buzz of sleep-deprivation spiked with liberal doses of caffeine accesses a state of consciousness shared by the vast majority of his Dev-land informants. Like many developers, he starts taking advantage of his flex hours, arriving to work at ten or later and hanging around for late-night pizza runs and gaming sessions, which in turn blur into even more and later nights spent with Freya and her housemates. Days run together, and the boundaries between work and not-work grow fuzzier with each passing week.

His yoga classes, however — undertaken at Freya's urging — constitute an entirely separate world. The instructor, a hunchbacked fifty-something woman who swears she'd be in a wheelchair by now if it weren't for her Practice, says that the primary goal of yoga is to create space. Physical space through bodily relaxation and flexibility, but also psychic space, both mental and spiritual. Nothing must be forced or pushed or strained. Step by slow step, she softly narrates her students' movements, and Matthew immerses himself in the kinaesthetic awareness of each pose. His body becomes a refuge, a vantage point from which to observe the mind. Eventually, says the instructor, the mind will settle on its own, just as muscles will stretch and gain flexibility with Practice. Correcting Matthew's *Warrior II*, she manually adjusts his hips. Then she pauses, steps back, and gives him a look he can't interpret.

"You have a *lot* of energy," she says.

He can't tell from her expression if this is a good or bad thing. But at the moment she says it, he knows it to be true. No doubt, no analysis, no questioning. He accepts the statement and continues his Practice.

His favourite pose is *savasana*, the corpse. Closing his eyes, he follows the seemingly nonsensical instructions to *soften the forehead* and *let the eyes sink into the head*. He feels each contour and crack in the plastic mat beneath him, smells the stale sweat accumulated through years of rec-centre use, hears the whisper of each adjacent student's breathing, sirens dopplering in the distance. Joints and muscles fall into place, twitching involuntarily with the release of accumulated tension. Waves of disconnected emotion surface: sadness, elation, fear, joy. Sourceless and transient, they wash over him and depart.

At these times, Matthew begins to sense the Presence directly, to feel it hovering just beneath the surface. And when he emerges from the pose, he invariably finds himself unwilling to interact with his classmates. In these moments he requires no further stimulation beyond the opening of his eyes, returning to a world revealed for the briefest of instants as entirely devoid of meaning, judgement, or Self.

As his sense of the Presence grows and various hidden worlds replace more and more of the everyday, Matthew finds that he no longer believes or disbelieves his own perceptions. All may be real, delusional, or (most likely) somewhere in between. Are "they" monitoring his electronic records? Yes, undoubtedly. But do "they" know (or care) what these records represent beyond the purely statistical? Probably not. Unless Anton or someone like him has taken a particular interest, which seems unlikely. And what of the proliferation of other, less material Hidden Worlds? Matthew now recognizes he will never know what really happened with El, or Billie, or any of the others. But he can choose to believe them. Or not.

Freya tells him story upon story. She says she did acid almost daily in grade twelve, but now saves it for special occasions, maybe once or twice a year. She describes the paradoxically addictive pleasure/pain of having her clitoris pierced and discusses her boyfriend's broad array of lovers as casually as she does her own. They discuss number theory, art, and music. Freya never says that she is a practising witch, or a member of a coven. But she does openly joke with one of her housemates.

"Hey, are you calling my friends witches?" she says, feigning outrage.

Then they laugh and laugh and laugh.

Freya leads Matthew through a maze of night-quiet residential streets to a narrow asphalt footpath between houses. He's lived in this area for years but has never before seen this path, nor is he familiar with half the streets they have walked down to get here. It's as if she's leading him into an alternate dimension, a parallel city within the city, a map unfolding recursively into folded, tesseracted space itself. The path emerges into heavily wooded greenspace, back yard fences disappearing as the asphalt ribbon meanders between tall deciduous trees and groomed topiary. Occasional lampposts cast a dappled illumination through overhanging branches, and Matthew glimpses shadowed headstones jutting like ancient megaliths from the glistening, dew-damp grass. At a fork in the path, Freya stops, sets down her bag, and sits cross-legged, inviting Matthew to join her.

She fishes the stash from her handbag and carefully arranges her implements: a half-full baggie, scissors, a dented zippo, and a small glass pipe. As she packs the pipe, she points out the closest trees on either side of the path, how the trunk on the left bifurcates two feet up from its base like a pair of spread legs, the one on the right three-split in the same way, the branches of both mingling overhead to form a low, leafy archway. She explains that the tree on the left is female, the one on the right male, and this spot at the centre represents a perfect balance-point between the two. Passing Matthew the lit pipe, she says she usually comes here alone.

Matthew inhales, holds the smoke in his lungs as he returns the pipe, closes his eyes, and slips directly into the mental state he associates with savasana. He feels the grit of cool asphalt beneath him, smells the green of fresh-cut grass, a hint of dark, freshly turned earth. He hears the lighter's flick, followed by a breathy hiss and a soft, smouldering crackle. Nothing else.

A fine and private place indeed.

He opens his eyes.

The light of the nearest lamppost illuminates little beyond the path itself, and the headstones barely visible between shadowy pillars of living wood project a muted endurance, the silent strength of stone. Trees and headstones, life and death, male and female, a splitting ribbon of asphalt overhung by a lattice of intertwining limbs. All of these forking paths, branching like quantum worldlines, remind Matthew of the Everett-Wheeler hypothesis.

In 1957, Hugh Everett argued that the most elegant solution to the problem of wave-function collapse was the postulation of multiple, branching worlds. If quantum collapse required the invention of additional, vague, and poorly understood entities to account for itself — such as the bizarrely influential "conscious" observer — then Occam's razor would suggest an alternative account. Perhaps, argued Everett, the wave-function never collapsed at all but merely continued to evolve undisturbed in mutually non-interfering (orthogonal) dimensions. Just as an observer in a physically accelerated frame of reference must invent an imaginary "centrifugal" force to account for anomalous results within that frame, so might a dimensionally limited observer be forced to invent a specious "conscious-observer" effect to explain the singular results of quantum measurement within a dimensionally limited world.

But if the observer (being a part of the world) also "split" along with the world, the apparently singular result of quantum measurement would in fact represent only one of many measured results by one of the many observers in one of many possible — and entirely real — worlds. And the only way that such multiple worlds could continue to interact, as in the case of an interference pattern, would be in the absence of discrete, deterministic measurement. In such a model, the presence of a conscious observer doesn't alter the universe; rather, the act of measurement limits the observer's consciousness. The wave-function doesn't *collapse*; the observer *splits*.

Matthew feels his wave-function spreading like a cloud across multiple worlds just as Freya, still facing him, spreads across additional worlds that overlap only indirectly with his own. Interference patterns and shadows, light filtered through leaves onto dappled asphalt. Matthew understands Freya's world no better (or worse) than any of the others who came before. But since he has not yet tried to measure her, they remain overlapping, not yet definitively split. So long as he can refrain from concrete measurement, the interference pattern will remain.

Matthew looks over to find Freya watching him. She leans forward, takes his hand, and holds it to her cheek so he can feel her smile.

"Yes," she says. "Yes, exactly."

They trace their winding path back through the shadowed graveyard to brighter residential streets. In a small municipal park, a merry-go-round sits abandoned next to a sandbox, monkey bars, and an adult-sized swing set. Unlike the graveyard, this park is unlit and open to the clear sky, the moonlight bright enough to cast sharp, distinct shadows. Freya leads Matthew to the swings, gestures for him to take one, then pauses and turns away. A small rustling disturbs the bushes. Freya opens her bag, takes out a candy bar, and breaks it into small pieces. Then she distributes these pieces in a line between her and the bushes, keeping a few in her hand and placing one on her shoulder as she settles to the grass and waits.

A squirrel emerges from the underbrush, moving in small, cautious fits and starts. Two hops. Freeze. Another hop, and it reaches the first piece, snatches it up, and dashes back to cover. When it re-emerges, it finds the second piece, a foot closer. This time it holds the candy between its forepaws, glancing frantically about in all directions and chewing quickly until the food is gone. Two more hops to the next piece, and another two to the next, until the squirrel is close enough that Freya could reach out and touch it if she chose.

She watches the squirrel, the squirrel watches her, and Matthew watches them both from his seat on the swings. A small, encouraging smile touches Freya's lips. One more hop, and the squirrel is eating from her hand. Another, and it sits perched on her far shoulder, retrieving the final piece. The squirrel leans in towards Freya's ear, as if whispering secrets. A witch and her familiar. Or an extremely patient animal lover feeding a squirrel.

This time, Matthew finds himself thinking of Tanya Luhrmann, a cultural anthropologist who studied occult practice in late twentieth-century England. According to Luhrmann, the highest level adepts invariably say they do not believe in magic. They practice it, certainly, but when it comes to *belief*, they maintain a perfect balance between absolute skepticism and empirical knowledge. On one hand, disbelief could indicate a deep cynicism, reducing magic to nothing more than an essentially psychological placebo effect. On the other, to not-believe could indicate a certainty so deep as to preclude belief entirely. One might choose not to believe in gravity, but apples will continue to fall from trees, regardless.

This, thinks Matthew, is the adept's version of the Everett-Wheeler hypothesis, possible worlds branching outwards in both directions, into the past as well as the future. This preservation of perfect ambiguity allows the contemporary creation of ancient rituals, alternative histories that are both invented and real. Create a ritual, bury authorship, invent a history, and soon enough that ritual and the history beneath it become real. According to Luhrmann, this is a well known, even encouraged practice in many occult communities. And since the adept does not *believe*, the apparent contradiction is of negligible importance.

The squirrel leaps down from Freya's shoulder and bounds off into the bushes. Freya dusts herself off and joins Matthew on the swings. Gravel scuffs as first Freya, then Matthew, both begin to swing, chain links creaking at their joints with each oscillation, the self-created breeze of their respective passages rushing in their ears. As they swing in alternating cycles, one forward then back, the other back then forward, Freya speaks.

"You know why I love the past?"

Matthew waits.

The two of them swing in perfect anti-synchrony for two more full cycles.

"I love the past," she says. "It's the only thing we can change."

NOTES

ON QUOTED AND PARAPHRASED MATERIALS

No writer works in a vacuum, and I would like to acknowledge the sources and materials listed below, all of which have contributed in various ways to the stories in this book.

The voice in the narrator's head in "Blackbird Shuffle (The Major Arcana)" quotes the title of "Happiness Is a Warm Gun" from the Beatles' self-titled album *The Beatles* (Apple Records, 1968).

The epigraph for "The Concept of a Photon" is quoted from *Science and Humanism: Physics in Our Time*, by Erwin Schrödinger (Cambridge University Press, 1951).

The epigraph for "The Smut Story (III)" is quoted from "Being One's Own Pornographer," by Candas Jane Dorsey, copyright © 1996, as published in *ParaDoxa*, volume 2, issue 2. Used by permission of the author.

Sebastian's quotations — and highly editorialized, second-hand paraphrases — of the DSM-IV in "Junk Mail" are drawn from the "Schizophrenia" entry in the *Diagnostic and Statistical Manual of Mental Disorders*, Fourth Edition, Text Revision (American Psychiatric Association, 2000).

Andrew's occasional quotations and paraphrases of Lao Tsu — who he refers to as simply "the sage" — in "The Mysterious East (Fredericton, NB)" are drawn from the *Tao Te Ching*, as translated by Gia-Fu Feng and Jane English (Vintage Books, 1972).

The two main books Matthew refers to in "The Everett-Wheeler Hypothesis" are Wade Davis's *The Serpent and the Rainbow*

(Simon and Schuster, 1985) and Tanya Luhrmann's *Persuasions of the Witch's Craft* (Harvard University Press, 1989). Like Matthew, I think these are both wonderful books; however, Matthew's (and El's) opinions and summaries of these texts are entirely their own.

ON PREVIOUSLY PUBLISHED VERSIONS OF THESE STORIES
Earlier versions of some of these stories appeared in a variety of journals and anthologies, and I am deeply grateful for each one. Thank you to the editors, magazines, and publishers who accepted and published the following pieces:

"Blackbird Shuffle (The Major Arcana)" appeared in *Prairie Fire* 25.4 (2004) and was later reprinted in *Tesseracts Ten* (Eds. Robert Charles Wilson and Edo van Belkom, Edge Science Fiction and Fantasy Publishing, 2006) and *Qwerty Decade* (Eds. Jill Connell and Joel Katelnikoff, Icehouse Press, 2006).

"The Concept of a Photon" appeared in *Prairie Fire* 28.2 (2007).

"Mindreader" appeared in *Qwerty* 15 (2004) and was reprinted in *The Neo-Comintern* 284 (2004).

"Junk Mail" appeared in *Prairie Fire* 26.2 (2005).

"The Mysterious East (Fredericton, NB)" appeared in *The Fiddlehead* 246 (2011), and an excerpt from an earlier draft of this story also appeared in *Hermen* 1 (2009).

An excerpt from an early draft of "The Everett-Wheeler Hypothesis" appeared in *Hermen* 2 (2010) under the title "The Garden of Forking Paths."

ACKNOWLEDGEMENTS

Thank you to everyone at Freehand. To JoAnn McCaig and the editorial board for taking a chance on the book, to Kelsey Attard for her patience with my long emails and incessant first-time-book-author questions (and for keeping us all on-track), to Natalie Olsen for the book design, and to Barbara Scott for pushing me to revise the hell out of these stories, even the ones I thought were long-since "finished." You were right. They're stronger now.

Thanks to my Edmonton writing communities, particularly to the Hermen reading series for which portions of some of these stories were originally drafted and performed. To Christine Weisenthal's creative nonfiction workshop, a godsend to any writer struggling to produce new work while simultaneously pursuing a PhD. It was a great class, with a great group of writers. To my Edmonton-writer posse, for workshopping, friendship, and general camaraderie along the way: Joel Katelnikoff, Jasmina Odor, Rebecca Frederickson. And to all the rest of the old Edmonton workshop too: Ben Lof, Barbara Romanik, Jill Connell, Naomi Lewis, and more. I learned from all of you.

Thanks to the Banff Writing Studio, where this collection originally turned the corner from being a bunch-of-stories-I-wrote to feeling more like a book. To my mentors there, Greg Hollingshead and Edna Alford, for their tremendous feedback, and to all the rest of the participants as well. There's something about a community of writers, and your collective successes since then have been an inspiration. Thanks also to the Alberta Foundation for the Arts, who funded my attendance to the Writing Studio and then, later, supported the final stages of writing this manuscript.

Thanks to the Frederictonians. To Mark Anthony Jarman for the feedback, the ruthless-in-a-good-way editing, that tremendous ability to simply *see* what was (or wasn't) working in a piece of writing, and far too many beers to count. To my old Fredericton thesis-writing group: Craig Davidson and Erin Tigchelaar. Clearly, we taught each other well.

Thanks to all the long-time friends I have met through the International Conference on the Fantastic in the Arts. There are so many that to name all of you would take a whole other set of acknowledgements. Still, thank you. Thanks especially to Isabella Van Elferen and Regina Hansen, who first encouraged me to "come out" as a writer at ICFA and whose enthusiasm, friendship, and occasional wagers have been an incredible source of motivation and support for years now. Such generosity of spirit is humbling.

Thanks to my family, who may at times have thought that I (and my stories) were a bit bonkers but were nonetheless supportive through it all. To all the old Waterloo writing workshops, off and on, in classes and out. Thanks especially to the instructor who gave me an A- on that urban fantasy story I wrote for his class, which later became my first paid publication. I wanted an A, dammit. That sense of dissatisfaction was a great motivator.

Finally, thanks to all the writers whose work has inspired me for as long as I can remember, from C.S. Lewis to Madeleine L'Engle to Ursula K. Le Guin to Angela Carter to David Mitchell to Sean Stewart to Candas Jane Dorsey to . . . Well, the list goes on. And to all the friends and readers who have been there along the way, backing me up, reading my stuff. That list keeps growing too. Thank you.

GREG BECHTEL's occasionally prize-winning stories have appeared in several journals and anthologies, including *The Fiddlehead*, *Prairie Fire*, *On Spec*, *Qwerty*, and the *Tesseracts* anthologies of Canadian speculative fiction. Originally from Kitchener-Waterloo, Ontario, Greg has lived at various times in Toronto, Deep River, Jamaica, Ottawa, Quebec City, and Fredericton while working (among other things) as a lifeguard, technical writer, mover, visual basic programmer, camp counsellor, semiconductor laser labtech, cab driver, tutor, and teacher. Currently, he lives and writes in Edmonton, where he teaches English Literature and Creative Writing at the University of Alberta whenever they let him. *Boundary Problems* is his first book. Feel free to drop him a line at blackbirdshuffle@gmail.com.